Tangled Mess

K.L. Middleton

Prologue

Ransom

I tipped the bottle of Patron back and took another swig, watching as the two girls rolled around in my king-sized bed, whimpering and moaning in pleasure as their tongues danced between the other's thighs. The scene was straight out of a porno – two gorgeous girls, both horny, and begging me to join them. It was a fantasy many guys would give their left nut for. Hell, it used to be mine. These days, however, it was just another Sunday night in my L.A. condo.

Or was it Monday?

The brunette, some famous lingerie model, raised her head, and gave me a sensuous smile. "Aren't you going to join us, Ransom?" she purred.

Trying to focus, I waved my hand at the blurred image. "Nah," I answered in a thick voice. "Gonna sit this one out."

She licked her full lips suggestively. "Are you sure? Or are we going to have to keep begging?"

I smiled lazily. "Not really sure of anything, sweetness."

She giggled, thinking I was flirting with her, and then resumed pleasuring the redhead

who was staring at me with hungry, adoring eyes.
I rubbed a hand over my face, trying to remember
what her name was.

Ginger? Cinnamon?

It really didn't matter. To me, Spice-Girl
was just another faceless groupie, one who'd
caught my eye during my drummer, Vance's,
birthday party, a few hours earlier. She'd been
wearing some kind of silver sequined halter-top,
her nipples poking through as she'd plopped
herself onto my lap, whispering kinky shit into
my ear, finally, offering to suck my cock. I
obliged, taking her up on the offer in the
bathroom, but in the end had to push her away. I
couldn't stay hard, looking down at a girl who
stared up at me like I was something I wasn't.

A god.

I was by no means a "god." Gods weren't
miserable, nor were they ruled by others.

Hell, I was both.

On the outside, my life was the stuff that
dreams were made of. I was a filthy rich,
celebrity, with hordes of women, drugs, and
alcohol at my disposal. I owned several cars, four
homes, a private jet, and a small island in the
Caribbean. I was *the* shit. An All-American-
Grammy-Winning-Rock Star.

Right, what a fucking joke...

I was a nothing but a prisoner, owned by
the small print in my contracts, and managers
who treated me like a child at twenty-five. I
wasn't allowed to write my own music, plan my
own tours, or make any more important decisions

about my life, let alone my career. Shit, I couldn't even step outside my front door without being monitored or chastised by one of my P.R. peeps. The only thing I could control was getting wasted, so I indulged as much as possible. As far as I was concerned, the fact that I still had control over what I did to my body was what kept me from drowning in their cesspool of non-negotiable rules. Or, hell, maybe it was pushing me under faster, I didn't even fucking know anymore. The shitty truth was that even if I wanted to walk away from all of the glory and stardom, my mug was plastered everywhere on magazines, television, billboards, and bathroom stalls. I couldn't go anywhere without being followed by reporters or star-struck fans. Hell, I needed bodyguards just to go to fucking McDonalds for a shake. Then, there were the crazy, obsessed stalkers who'd sworn an undying love for me, convinced that we were soul-mates. Or the other fanatics who just simply wanted to destroy me.

Why?

I was Ransom, an icon to some, the epitome of sin and debauchery to others. In reality, I was a puppet with too many strings and no Blue Fairy in sight.

Chapter One

Tiffany

"Tiff!" hollered Sinclair. "Are you almost ready? We're going to be late!"

My hands trembled as I stared blindly into the mirror, trying not to throw up. In just a matter of two hours I'd gone from giddy, to being terrified beyond belief. I wasn't foolish enough to believe that it was going to get any better, either. Not in the next couple of hours, at least.

You can still back out, I thought, tapping my foot on the ground nervously. *Save yourself from being humiliated or snickered at.*

She knocked on the door. "Sweetie?"

I sighed and stood up straight. *Oh, hell, I can't let Sinclair down.*

"I'm ready," I said, opening the door.

"You look awesome," she said, taking a step back and nodding.

"Thanks," I replied, stepping over Felix, who glared up at me with loathing. I narrowed my eyes and scowled back. "You're cute, but don't think I've forgotten that it's all a disguise."

"I guess he has to 'go'," said Sinclair, smiling with amusement down at her cat.

Felix.

He was the only cat I knew that used a toilet and had little tolerance for others using *his* bathroom. Sinclair had somehow trained him to use it when he was a kitten, and I'd made the mistake of walking in on him a few months ago. He'd growled at me and then the little turd had peed on my new designer purse, his message clear. Although I'd wanted nothing more than to drop him off of the balcony, I'd held my cool, which was good because the next day, Sinclair had went and replaced the three-hundred dollar purse I'd saved all spring for.

Felix rubbed up against Sinclair and then strutted like royalty into the bathroom.

I rolled my eyes.

"I like that outfit," she said, nodding in approval. "You now look like a mixture between a country singer and a rock star."

"You think so?" I asked, biting my lower lip.

"Hell yes, I think so. You should, too," she said, adjusting one of my curls. "Take it from me, you already look like a star."

I thought I looked more like Cowgirl Barbie, but I kept that to myself. Sinclair had spent hours curling my blonde hair and applying my makeup with detailed precision. With my shaky hands, I would have never been able to pull anything off, if it wasn't for her. "Well, thanks for all of your help," I answered. "I just wish I wasn't so damn nervous."

"Why? Girl, you look beautiful, sexy, and ready to take on the world."

I chuckled. "Well, looks are deceiving."

"Yes, but your voice isn't. Once you open up that mouth of yours and start singing, they're going to be blown away."

"And what if I'm too nervous to sing?"

She touched my shoulder. "You won't be. Just calm down, Tiffany. You look great and your voice is amazing." She tilted her head and nodded. "In fact, you look like the girl-next-door. The judges will love it."

After combing through my closet several times on this last minute decision, I'd settled on a short denim skirt, a plain white blouse with a blue camisole, and distressed brown cowgirl boots.

Sinclair straightened the silver locket around my neck. "I'm sure this will give you luck, too."

I reached up and touched my mother's locket. She'd given it to me in the hospital three years ago, right before she'd died from a rare type of breast cancer. Inside of it was a picture of my beautiful, golden-haired parents on their wedding day. Unfortunately, five years after that photo, my father had been killed by a drunk driver. From what my mother had explained, he'd been jogging early one Saturday morning around my third birthday, when someone had hit him, leaving my mother a devastated widow at the age of twenty-eight. Fortunately for me, my mother had pulled through a short stint of depression, determined to make sure I grew up in an atmosphere filled with laughter and love.

And she had.

She'd raised me all on her own, while going to college and working on the weekends at a nearby convenience store. Eventually, she'd graduated and started teaching History to high school students, which she'd adored. Then, after I graduated from senior high and started beauty school, she was diagnosed with cancer, and I lost her shortly afterwards. But, she never complained. Not even through all of the chemo treatments. In fact, as far as I could remember, she'd always cherished life, making me the center of hers. I only wished she was here now to help calm my nerves, like she had so many times in the past.

"Are you *really* that nervous?" asked Sinclair, grabbing a brush from her purse. She ran it through her long, auburn hair and I stared at her, wishing I was as self-confident as she was. Looking like a super-model and having a rich boyfriend, obviously, didn't hurt.

"Very. I'll probably make a complete fool out of myself and get thrown out."

She chuckled. "You're going to knock them dead, Tiff. They're going to look into those big, blue eyes, hear that beautiful voice of yours, and be completely blown away. I only wish I could watch it happen."

I snorted. "Right."

She turned to me, grabbed my shoulders, and shook me playfully. "Stop thinking that way. You have to go in there, and believe that *you* and you *alone*, will be the next 'American Icon'. I have total faith in you."

American Icon, a realty-show-slash-singing-competition that traveled around the U.S. in search of its next big star. The winner would be given a record contract and two-million dollars upfront. It had already launched the careers of six lucky people, who were now so rich and successful, they'd become household names.

I smiled sheepishly. "I wish I had your confidence."

"Just stop thinking like that. In fact, I know this is a stupid cliché, but if you're really that freaked out, just try to imagine the judges in their underwear. Seriously."

I laughed. "Right, with my luck the judges will be hot and I'll be drooling."

"Okay, even better. Pretend that they *are* your lovers as you're singing and then you can seduce those votes right out of them."

I opened up a bottle of water and shook my head. "Easy for you to say. I still can't believe I let you talk me into this."

"When you're rich and famous, you're going to thank the hell out of me. Now, let's go before we keep Jesse waiting and he throws a hissy fit."

I raised my eyebrows. "Jesse's driving?"

"He insisted that he drive when he heard the news. He's hoping to meet Taylor Blake."

Taylor Blake, the host for American Icon, *was* hot. He also had the reputation for being a total scoundrel when it came to women. Rumor had it that he went through more women than hair gel.

"Does Jesse know what he's getting himself into?" I asked, thinking back to the long lines of contestants they always showed on television.

"Yeah, he said so. He also said that it was better than watching paint dry. Literally. I guess Daniel is painting Jesse's new house, and he needed an excuse to escape. You know Jesse, he hates any kind of physical labor. He's afraid of getting dirt under his nails."

"I'm sure. So, how are those two lovebirds doing?"

"Fine, I guess," said Sinclair. "Although, Jesse has been complaining about Daniel's suggestion that they go on an Alaskan cruise."

"Why would he complain about that?"

"He said something about it being a floating retirement home, and didn't want any old coots checking him out."

"Seriously? He said that?"

She nodded. "Jesse is sweet, but he's also very vain."

"Well, he's certainly good-looking, so I can kind of understand it."

"I know, but I'm sure it isn't easy to live with, at least not for Daniel. Anyway, you ready to go?" she asked, grabbing her keys from the coffee table.

No...

I swallowed the lump of fear in the back of my throat. "I suppose."

She grabbed my hand and pulled me towards the door. "Relax. This is going to be fun."

I stopped abruptly. "Wait."

Her green eyes narrowed. "What?"

"I... I just don't think I can really do this," I squeaked.

"Yes, you can."

I shook my head vehemently. "No, seriously, I think I'm going to throw up if I try and go through with this."

She stared at me in alarm. "Don't you dare, you'll ruin your makeup."

I backed away from her. "I... I can't do this, Sinclair. I'm sorry for wasting your time this morning."

She raised her finger. "You can do this, and do you know why?"

I opened my mouth to protest but she went on.

"Because God gave you that voice for a reason. As far as I'm concerned, it was a gift, one that was meant to be shared with the world. Now, you're going to march in front of those judges with your head held high. Then you're going to open up your mouth and make their jaws drop. I swear to you, this is your destiny, your moment to shine, I can just feel it. Now, buck-up, honey, because I'm not letting you miss this chance. It might not ever come again."

I blushed. "You really believe that?"

"Of course I do and I don't know what else I can really say to make you believe it, too."

"You don't have to say anything else," I replied, clutching my purse tighter. "Let's just go and do this before I change my mind again."

"Good. Um, by the way," she smiled sheepishly. "I heard that Ransom is one of the judges, and I want you to try to get his autograph."

My throat went dry. "Ransom?"

"Yes. I told my friend I'd somehow get it for her daughter. She's totally in love with that guy."

"Ransom?" I said, still not quite believing it.

She nodded. "Yeah, isn't that great? He's one of the original Icon winners. Plus, he's from California. One of our own homeboys."

"No. It's not *that* great," I said, setting my purse down.

"Why?"

"Because," I replied. "I was really good friends with his sister, and let's just say that he's a total jerk. I'll never win if Ransom is one of the judges."

Her jaw dropped. "You actually *know* Ransom?"

"Unfortunately," I said, remembering the way he used to tease and call me "Tiffy Taffy" or just plain "Taffy" for short. He also used to chase us around with water guns, and terrorize us at night during sleepovers.

"Wow," she said, shaking her head in disbelief. "You lucky girl."

I snorted. "Believe me, there was no luck involved. Anyway, I'm sure there must be some kind of rule against knowing one of the judges."

"When was the last time you saw him?"

I shrugged. "I guess I was about fourteen."

"Fourteen?" She waved her hand. "Oh hell, he probably won't even remember you."

"He'll remember, believe me," I said, thinking back to the last time we'd been together.

I'd made a fool out of myself, and the thought of facing him was making me more ill than the contest itself.

"You weren't friends, though, right?"

"Right."

"So, who cares if you knew him. You weren't friends, and nobody needs to know that you were friends with his sister. Besides, he has met so many people being famous, he might not recognize you."

"Let's hope not."

"Wow. I still can't believe you knew Ransom," said Sinclair, smirking. "What are the odds of that?"

"What about Ransom?" asked Jesse, walking through the door. "And what's taking you girls so long? I have the top down, and this heat is fucking up my hair."

Sinclair walked over to him and began fussing with his drooping hair. "We were just leaving," she said. "Did you know that Tiffany knew Ransom growing up?"

His eyes widened. "You're kidding? You knew Ransom?"

I shrugged. "A little."

He took off his sunglasses and cleaned them with the edge of his shirt. "I'd love to get my hands on that hunk. He is so freaken *yummy*. I met him at one of my parents' parties, and let me just say this – he's even more gorgeous in person."

"We used to call him 'Handsome Ransom', growing up," I said and then smiled. "He didn't care for it too much."

"Seriously? It's a compliment," said Sinclair.

"Well, it embarrassed him back then," I said. "He was pretty modest about his looks back in those days."

"He obviously grew out of that. The guy is a legend now," replied Sinclair.

"In more ways than one," said Jesse.

"What do you mean?" I asked.

He smirked. "Let's just say he's pretty rowdy these days. Don't you read the papers?"

Sinclair pushed her hair behind her ears. "You mean those gossip tabloids?"

"They're not all gossip," said Jesse. "I believe the stories about Ransom. I mean, there are just *too* many of them to all be false."

"Honestly, it wouldn't surprise me," I said. "He was trouble growing up, and I'm sure with all of his money and fame, there's nothing to stop Ransom from being an all-out hell raiser."

We walked out of the apartment and Sinclair locked the door.

"I know one thing," said Jesse with a wicked grin. "That deep, sexy voice of his raises more than just a little hell for me; too bad he's straight."

He was definitely straight. In fact, I'd never forget the look in his eyes right before I'd kissed him.

It had been at his graduation party. His sister Remy and I had snuck some beer and gotten pretty tipsy. She'd left at some point, to pass out in her bedroom, while I'd played cards with some of Ransom's hot friends in the den. When he'd wandered in and noticed what was happening, he'd pulled me away from the table, down through the hallway to the guest bedroom, and proceeded to chew me out. I could still remember the fire in his eyes that night.

"What in the hell were you thinking?" he'd barked, angrier than I'd ever seen him.

I'd raised my chin. "I was just playing cards. What's the big deal?"

"It wasn't just cards. Obviously, you've been drinking."

"I don't know what you're talking about," I'd lied.

His slate-grey eyes had burned into mine. "Stay away from those guys, Taffy. They don't care how old you are and I don't want you getting hurt."

Not understanding exactly what he was getting at, I'd placed my hands on my hips and looked at him defiantly. "That's exactly the point," I said. "They don't treat me like a child. Not like *you* do."

He rolled his eyes. "You *are* still a child. You're what... fifteen, sixteen?"

I didn't tell him I was fourteen. "I'm not a child and... I have a boyfriend who... kisses me. In fact, I've done a lot of things."

A look of surprise and then amusement had spread across his face. "Oh, is that so?"

He had me backed up into a corner and was so close that I'd never noticed how perfectly sculpted his jawline was or how full his lips were. "Yes, so you see, I'm *not* a little girl anymore."

He'd stared at my mouth, making my tummy fluttery and warm. "You may not look like it, but you are, Taffy."

My heart had pounded madly in my chest as I'd imagined what it would feel like if our lips touched. I'd kissed a couple of boys already, but none of them had been as handsome, or as experienced as Ransom. Still pretty tipsy, I'd decided to be daring, like the girls in my teen romance books. Standing on my tiptoes, I'd slid my hands around his neck, and crushed my lips against his.

Groaning, he'd kissed me back for a couple of seconds, until our tongues touched. Then he'd stiffened up, pushing me away. "Whoa, what in the hell are you doing, Taffy?"

Horrified and humiliated that he'd rejected me, I'd taken off before the tears had fallen. We hadn't seen each other since.

Chapter Two

Ransom

The loud pounding on my bedroom door almost matched the horrible one wreaking havoc in my head.

"Ransom!" hollered my agent, Sonia Jenkins, from the other side of the door. "Get your ass out of bed and get dressed! Now!"

"Hold on," I muttered, trying to ignore the all-too familiar nausea and heartburn. I sat up and reached for the bottle of ibuprofen and Rolaids on my nightstand. The unexpected rustle of silk sheets startled me.

"Hey, Ransom," smiled a strange brunette, stretching out next to me.

Normally I kicked them out before I passed out. This one had apparently slipped through the cracks. I cleared my throat. "Oh, hey... listen, Susie. You've got to get dressed and leave."

Her face darkened. "It's Sara."

I grinned. "Sorry, Sara. Come on, you've really got to hustle. You don't want to be in here when Sonia rips me a new asshole." My head was beginning to clear, and I was now just remembering how I'd fucked up big-time this morning. I was supposed to be on the set of American Icon an hour ago.

The girl stood up, stark naked, and I felt my cock twitch. She bent down and picked up a

lacy purple thong. "At least *something* got
fucked," she mumbled, under her breath.

Apparently, I'd been too drunk to perform.
Too bad it bothered her more than me. "Sorry,
Cindy," I said. "Maybe next time I won't have
such a whisky dick."

"It's Sara," she said, this time with a bright
smile. "So, you're really going to call me?"

"Of course," I lied.

She snapped the front of her bra. "Good,
because my friends had warned me about you; I
didn't want to believe it, though. I mean, you were
a complete gentleman last night."

I had to admit, I was always a nice guy
when I was shitfaced. Booze seemed to take the
edge off, most of the time. I wondered what her
definition of a complete gentleman was, though.
I'd obviously talked her into sex.

I stood up and tossed her the pink
camisole next to my feet. "Thanks."

She caught it and grimaced. "This isn't
mine," she said, dropping it quickly.

"Oh, sorry," I replied, pulling up my jeans.

Usually the *help* took care of forgotten
articles of clothing, but Brandy, the new maid,
had more than likely been the owner of the pink
camisole. I vaguely remember her lips around my
cock and my hands on her tits, before I'd taken
off for the club last night.

"Ransom!" yelled Sonia. "Dammit, we don't
have time. Get your shit together!"

I zipped up my jeans, walked over to the bedroom door, and opened it. "Sorry, Sonia, I totally forgot."

She glared at me. "Same excuse. What part of 'getting your career back in order' do you not understand? Nobody is going to want anything to do with you if you keep pulling this shit."

I ran a hand through my dark brown hair. "Do I have enough time to shower?"

She wrinkled her nose. "No. But you'd better. You smell like a mixture of tequila and a used tampon wrapped in fish guts."

Just then Sara, wearing a tight black dress and sexy red stilettos, sashayed over to us, and then pressed her lips to mine. "I think he smells awesome," she said with a wink. "Bye, sexy."

"Later, doll," I answered, watching her hips sway as she exited. One thing was for certain, even roaring drunk, I still ended up with the sexy ones. I wondered if I'd be so lucky without the fame.

Sonia snorted. "Jesus, Ransom. I hope you're using condoms."

I chuckled. She was crass, bossy, and never took shit from anyone, including me. She was also a die-hard lesbian, and I *loved* fucking with her. "I think I may have saved a couple. Want to join me in the shower?"

"You couldn't handle a woman like me, Ransom. My pussy would chew you up, and spit you out."

I cringed. "Jesus, I think my dick just crawled up into my stomach."

"Good. Now take your shower before I beat the hell out of you. I'm seriously pissed off right now, Ransom. This shit of yours isn't doing either of us any favors."

I sighed. "Sorry."

Truth of the matter was, I hadn't really thought about Sonia. Obviously, she took a lot of the heat for me. I owed her big time.

She pulled out her cell phone and waved me towards the bathroom. "Just get your ass moving."

An hour later, we were pulling up to the "Icon" audition site where thousands of people were already lined up. "Jesus," I said, reaching for the bottle of rum I had stashed inside of the limo. "Don't these people have lives?"

Sonia slapped my hand away from the bottle. "No drinking today. And no, many of them don't have the kind of life they want. That's why they're here."

I sat back and stared out the window. "They have no fucking clue."

"What was that?"

"You heard me," I replied, stretching out my legs. "This lifestyle isn't all it's cracked up to be. It looks good from the outside, but it's kind of tiring, if you ask me."

"Oh, quit being such a fucking pussy. You have everything. Fame, fortune, women waiting in line to lick your balls, and yet you're still complaining. What in the hell is wrong with you?"

"Yeah, and all I had to do was trade my soul."

She rolled her eyes. "Bullshit."

"I don't even know who I am anymore. I mean, shit, I have no fucking freedom."

She waved her hand. "I don't know what's gotten into you lately, but you're talking nonsense."

"Seriously, what if I wanted to fly off to... to... Hawaii? Tonight and without any security?"

She pushed the button on her pen several times, staring at me like I was completely nuts. "You know very well that you can't leave L.A. right now. You have too many responsibilities. Like it or not."

"Okay, what if I wanted to travel somewhere secluded, where nobody really knows me, after this 'American Icon' shit is completed? And I'm not talking about that island I purchased six months ago."

She shook her head. "This show is going to last about three to four months. Then, we have that European tour. It's already set up."

I narrowed my eyes. "And what if I don't want to tour?"

She leaned forward. "We talked about this weeks ago. You just recorded all of those new songs. You *have to* tour, Ransom. Everything has been arranged."

I sneered. "See? No freedom."

"Jesus Christ. Most guys would give their right nut to be in your position. What in the hell has gotten into you?"

The limo stopped and our driver got out.

"I'm just tired of it all. I mean, fuck, my entire life is being planned out by everyone else but me."

"That's because you're too irresponsible to handle it all yourself. Maybe if you'd get your drinking under control, things would be different."

"Drinking? Right. This shit started long ago, when I signed away my rights with Icon."

"Signed away? Listen, this isn't just about you, Ransom. Too many people are counting on the success of your albums. Your band, the lives of their families, all of your sponsors, and hell, even me. When you fuck up, you're not only hurting yourself, you're hurting all of us."

The limo driver opened my door, and I got out without answering. Everything she said was true, and it was ultimately why I stayed, and just didn't disappear. The band counted on me. They were my brothers, and I owed it to them.

As I was escorted towards the back entrance, a reporter asked me when I was touring in the U.S. again, and then thrust her microphone into my face.

I gave her a cocky grin. "Not sure. They haven't told me yet."

Doug, one of my bodyguards, blocked another reporter and barked, "Stay back!"

The media was everywhere as security quickly surrounded me, and I was ushered towards the building.

"Ransom," hollered a female reporter. "Are you late?"

"Ransom," yelled another one. "Partying all night, *again?*"

"Come on now, drugs and alcohol are bad," I yelled as I entered the building. "Everyone knows that."

"You're so full of shit," said Sonia.

"That hurts," I said, putting a hand on my heart. "Why are you so cruel?"

She looked past me. "Here comes the shit-storm."

I turned around just as Joe, one of the show's producers, rushed towards me. "Hurry, and get him into makeup," he growled, glaring at me.

"Hey, Joe."

"Jesus, do you have any idea of the shit you've caused because you're late? One more time, Ransom, and that's it. We'll find someone else."

"Sorry. My alarm didn't go off this morning."

His lips thinned. "Your alarm..."

"I'll get a new one," I said with a straight face. "Have my eye on this Mickey Mouse model."

His eyes blazed with anger. "Stop the fucking bullshit, and get your ass ready."

I saluted him, and then stepped into the dressing room they'd assigned me. A half hour later, I was ushered to the football field and a long table, where the other two celebrity judges sat waiting.

"Where in the hell have you been?" asked Tyrone Farr, a talented R&B artist who was also a record producer.

"Flat tire," I said, sitting on the other side of Deidra Swan, the third judge. "It was a bitch getting those lug nuts off, let me tell you."

"Hello, Ransom," smiled Deidra. She was British, married to a famous country singer, and had helped to launch the careers of many artists in the last twenty years. I actually had a great deal of respect for her. "So happy you could join us."

I knew she was also irritated, but wouldn't hold it against me. She was a fan favorite on Icon, and as sweet as they came. It was why she was one of the judges. She had a heart of gold, and always voted for the underdog when they had even a spark of talent.

I held out my hand. "It's my honor to finally meet you, Mrs. Swan."

"Oh... you can call me Deidra," she answered, shaking my hand. "And the feeling is mutual, young man. Now, be a dear, and try to be on time from now on."

I smiled. "To see that beautiful smile of yours again, I'll not only be here, but I'll have breakfast waiting. Do you prefer bagels or muffins?"

Her blue eyes sparkled. "Oh, I see it's true what they say about you," she said, releasing my hand.

I tilted my head. "What is that?"

"That your bullshit could fill up this stadium," interrupted Tyrone.

"Oh, Tyrone," sighed Deidra. "Play nice." She turned back to me. "The rumor is that you're a real charmer, and the women *adore* you."

I chuckled. "Well, I don't know about that."

"Of course you do," she said. "That's why you get away with so much. Then there's that sultry voice of yours. The female audience can't seem to get enough of you."

"Why do you think they brought him in?" stated Tyrone, with a sneer. "It wasn't for his punctuality, or his wit."

I scratched my jaw, wishing I would have had time to shave the itchy stubble. "What's your problem, man? So, I'm a little late. You don't have to be a fucking dick about it."

"You're the one being a fucking dick," said Tyrone. "One who's selfish and irresponsible. But we all expected that out of *Ransom*." He smiled humorlessly. "At least you're predictable, man."

"Is that right?" I asked in a bored voice.

"It is, so do us all a favor, and grow the fuck up."

"Settle down, boys," said Deidre. "We're going live soon."

"That's right," said Joe, walking towards us. "So we need you all ready. If you *are* going to argue, save it for the cameras. The audience loves drama."

"Shit," said Tyrone. "It's not even worth it."

"Live in four minutes!" hollered one of the cameramen. "Where's Taylor?"

"He's on the other side of the field interviewing some of the first contestants," replied another guy on the set.

"Someone go and get him," said Joe. He turned back to us. "Now, remember, millions of people are going to be watching, so be professional but keep it entertaining. Tyrone, you do what you do best, be a critical prick, Deidra, you keep the audience on your side, and Ransom... I want you to charm the pants off of the women. Even the fucking scary ones who can't sing worth shit and look like descendants of Sasquatch."

"Anything for you, Joe," I said. The truth was I just wanted to get this bullshit over with.

Taylor appeared shortly with his makeup artist, who prepped him as we glared at each other with mutual loathing. When she was finished powdering his face, he swaggered over.

"Ransom," he said, breaking the tense silence between us.

"Taylor," I answered, wrinkling my nose. "Did you step in shit, or is that your cheap-ass cologne I smell in the air?"

His lips thinned. "Your sister picked it out."

"I guess anything smells better than your au-naturel," I replied.

"At least my au-naturel doesn't reek of stale whiskey," he said.

"It's stale Tequila, Taylor," I said. "You should recognize that smell from the stripper's navel you licked clean last weekend."

"Don't start with the guilt trip, Ransom, it was my bachelor party."

"Oh, you remembered? I'd thought maybe you'd forgotten that you were actually getting married."

Taylor was engaged to my younger sister, and I couldn't stand the prick. He'd cheated on her at least once, but because it had been before they were engaged, Remy had given him another chance. Then, during his bachelor party, he'd disappeared with a stripper for fifteen minutes, and from the satisfied look on his face, along with her disappointed one, it was obvious he'd pulled his dick out.

"We are live in thirty seconds!" hollered the director.

"Oh, my," whispered Deidra, as Taylor walked away, "not much love between you two, is there?"

"He's a douchebag," I said under my breath. "The only thing I love about him is that he lives in another state."

While I lived in California, Taylor and Remy shared a penthouse in New York.

Tyrone chuckled. "You just earned some respect, cuz," he said, running a finger along his goatee. "I can't stand that prick, either. Guy is a slippery as they come. He's engaged to your sister?"

"Yep."

He shook his head. "Oh, man... that's fucked up. You have my condolences, man.

Hopefully your sister will see him for what he really is, and kick his ass to the curb.”

“Agreed.”

The familiar music started, we went live, and less than an hour later, life got a little more interesting.

Chapter Three

Tiffany

The audition lines were longer than any of us had expected. Wondering if it was a sign, I tried backing out again, but Sinclair wouldn't have it.

"You had to have expected this," she said. "This show attracts every fruit-loop in the city, and not just the talented ones."

"I know, but..."

"This is a once in a lifetime chance and you can't let a crowd like this intimidate you, hon. Besides, Jesse knows someone who can get us in right away," she said as we got out of the car.

Jesse re-tucked the bottom of his plaid blue and white shirt into his jeans. "That's right, because there's no way in hell I'd wait all day among all of those freaks, even for you, Tiffany."

"You'd better call your friend," said Sinclair.

He pulled out his phone as we started walking out of the parking towards the large coliseum, where the tryouts were being held. Lines of people surrounded the building and went all the way to the edge of the parking lot.

"Okay," said Jesse, hanging up. "We're supposed to go around to the back of the building, and my guy, Phillip, will get us in."

I raised my eyebrows. "It's that easy?"

"I don't know about easy. More like, expensive. I now owe him several drinks and a steak dinner this weekend," said Jesse.

"Seriously?" I said. "Let me buy, Jesse. It's the least I can do."

"Honey," said Jesse. "The bill will be over a grand by the time we're finished, so don't worry about it. Sinclair and I have it covered."

Sinclair's eyebrows shot up. "Excuse me?"

"A grand?" I gasped. "For dinner and drinks?"

"Yeah, and Sinclair is going to sweet talk my brother into joining us. Reed in turn, will feel like he has to pay because he's pussy-whipped, and will want to impress Sinclair, and yes a grand because Phillip won't expect anything less."

"What if Reed and I already have plans?" asked Sinclair.

Jesse smirked. "You can get your asses out of bed to eat."

"You're a sick guy, Jesse," she replied.

He cocked an eyebrow. "Tell me I'm wrong."

She shook her head and smiled.

"How's Reed doing, by the way?" I asked. "I haven't heard you mention him all week."

"He's doing fine," she replied. "Actually, he's been working a lot of long hours lately. Some big case that he can't discuss."

From the pensive look on her face, something was definitely bothering her.

"Have you guys found a place yet?" I asked. I knew they'd been talking about moving in together for the past couple of months.

She snorted. "Are you kidding? He barely has time to call me let alone go looking for a house."

"It's that bad?" I asked.

"Yes. I mean, we meet for lunch a few times a week, but it's not the same."

"Have you met his new assistant, Nina?" asked Jesse.

Sinclair frowned. "The blonde with the big boobs? How can anyone miss her?"

"I personally don't care for her," said Jesse. "Every time I call him at the office, she puts me on hold for such a long time, I wonder if she's doing it on purpose."

"She does it to me, too," said Sinclair. "It drives me crazy. Reed said he'd talk to her about it. Now I just call his cellphone."

"Is she respectful towards you in person?" asked Jesse.

"She's always been nice. I mean, I don't think I have anything to worry about, if that's what you're getting at."

"Reed adores you," I said. "You can tell by the way he looks at you."

"I... I know."

"He loves you, Sin," replied Jesse. "He hasn't been this faithful with anyone before. Well, he was with his ex, until he met you. But that says a lot. Believe me, he's been bitten by the love bug."

"I wouldn't go that far. He's never actually told me he loved me."

"Have you told him?" asked Jesse.

She smiled sheepishly. "No, I guess not."

"Do you?" I asked.

She blushed. "Yes, definitely."

"That's what I thought," I said. "Maybe if you told him first? You guys have been together for a while now. I guess I'm kind of surprised you never told him."

She shrugged. "I guess I just didn't want to scare him away."

"If that scares him away, then good riddance," replied Jesse. "Brother or not, I'm rooting for you, Sin."

"Thanks," she said.

As we started rounding the building, many of the other contestants were beginning to take notice of us.

"Where *you* going, sexy?" hollered a tall dark-skinned, cross-dresser who was beaming at Jesse.

"Far way, thank God," said Jesse under his breath. He looked at Sinclair. "That dress is gaudy, and those purple platform shoes are grotesque on those big feet. He gives transvestites a bad name."

"Wait!" the person yelled, moving out of line towards us. "Wait, a minute!"

"Oh no," groaned Jesse. "Why did God have to make me so damn hot?"

"Jesse! Don't you remember me?"

We stopped walking, and Jesse's eyes widened in recognition. "Oh, Yolanda! Girlfriend, I didn't recognize you with the blonde wig."

Yolanda stopped and threw his arms around Jesse. "We've missed you down at the club! Where've you been?"

"Oh, here and there," he answered, stepping back. "I have a new man, you know. We've been... busy."

"I heard," replied Yolanda, staring down at us with her heavily made-up face. Unfortunately, he didn't make a very attractive woman. There were too many angles in his face, and he didn't know the first thing about applying makeup. He was also very tall, almost seven feet with the platforms. "So, who are your friends? Are they competing?"

Jesse introduced us, and then looked towards the back of the building. "Look, we really have to go."

Yolanda's eyes narrowed. "Jesse, what are you up to? Did you get a special pass inside or something?"

"Actually, I have this friend who we're meeting –"

"You're getting in another way, aren't you?" he said, lowering his voice. "I know you've got connections all over Hollywood."

"Well –"

"Get me in too, please," he begged. "I can't wait out here all day. My makeup is already beginning to run."

"I really can't," said Jesse. "My hands are tied."

Yolanda's eyes grew large. "Jesse, if you don't get me in, I'm going to tell everyone about that time in Vegas, when you were so drunk, you..."

"Follow us," he interrupted, his voice clipped.

Yolanda winked at us as Jesse walked ahead.

Sinclair grinned at me. "I'll get it out of him later."

"It must be really bad," I whispered.

"I know. I can't wait to hear," she replied as we followed Yolanda and Jesse.

When we made it to the back of the building, an extremely attractive guy, who reminded me of Matt Damon, was standing by the entrance, looking nervous.

"Come on," he waved. "We have to hurry."

"Oh, look at that yummy morsel," murmured Yolanda, fluttering his eyelashes as he stepped closer to Phillip.

Phillip frowned and pointed towards Yolanda. "Who is this? I thought you said it was just going to be you and two girls?"

"Um, I need to get Yolanda in too, Phillip," whispered Jesse.

"Oh, no," he said shaking his head vehemently. "It was hard enough getting Tiffany in. Which one of you is Tiffany?"

I waved at him.

He nodded in approval. "Okay, we have to hurry. You're almost up."

"Whoa... what about me?" asked Yolanda.

"Sorry, you'll have to go to the end of the line," said Phillip. "I can't help you."

He put a hand on his hip and shook his finger at Phillip. "Hell no. You get me in or I'll grab one of those reporters outside, and tell them y'all are cheating."

"Yolanda..." groaned Jesse. "What the hell?"

"What the hell, nothing. I don't want to wait around all day, either. Now, what's it going to be? You going to get me in, or what?"

"Oh, fine," sighed Phillip, staring at his clipboard. "I'll figure something out. Just get inside."

We followed Phillip into the building, through a locker room, and then back outside to the football field.

"This way," ordered Phillip, moving quickly towards a large group of contestants. "Here is your entry information," he said, handing me a large card. "Now, the very first tryout is with one of the casting directors," he said, pointing to a line of several tables of men and women. "You have thirty seconds to 'wow' one of them, and then, if you pass, you'll be sent to the other side of the field, where the celebrity judges will determine if you can go any further in the competition."

I looked over to the other side of the field, which was surrounded by security, where the real action was taking place. Cameras were already rolling as finalists stood before the celebrity judges. Although I couldn't see him from this distance, I knew that Ransom was there. I could almost feel his presence in the pit of my stomach.

Crap.

"Okay," I replied.

"You *can* sing, can't you?" he asked. "I mean you look the part, thank goodness. But can you carry a tune?"

"So I've been told," I said.

I knew others enjoyed hearing me sing, especially my mother when she was still alive. After she'd been diagnosed with cancer and had to go through chemo, I'd made a CD for her, which she'd played during her treatments. She'd said that listening to me always made everything a little more bearable.

"So, have you ever had any singing lessons?" he asked.

"No, but I was in the church choir for several years," I said.

He sighed. "But you've never had any voice lessons?"

"Oh, she has a fantastic voice," said Jesse, who'd never heard me sing before. "She's going all the way, you'll see, Phillip."

"I just don't want to waste my time here," he said. "I'm risking my ass getting you in front of all the other contestants."

I smiled gratefully. "And I appreciate it."

"I have a voice, too," said Yolanda. "I've been told that I sound like Whitney Houston or Beyonce."

Phillip wrinkled his nose. "Really?"

"That's right. Now, where's my entry card?" ask Yolanda.

"Patience," he replied. "I'll get you one in a few minutes."

"You'd better," said Yolanda, glancing down at his long red nails. "I want to go and have my nails filled this afternoon, so the sooner I'm up, the better."

"Be ready, Tiffany," replied Phillip, ignoring Yolanda. "You're almost up. Just watch the screen for your number."

"Thanks, Phillip," I replied.

He nodded and walked away with Yolanda on his heels.

"Ready, honey?" asked Sinclair.

I blew out a long breath. "I think so. I'm just still so freaking nervous."

"You'll do great," she said. "I have faith in you."

"Do you need any water or anything?" asked Jesse. "I can try and find you something."

Sinclair reached into her oversized purse. "I brought some."

"I wish I was as prepared as you were," I said to Sinclair as she handed me the bottle. "How do you feel about auditioning for me?"

"Would you like to lose?" smirked Jesse. "Sinclair couldn't hold a note if she tried."

She nodded. "This is true."

"Isn't that your number?" asked Jesse, staring up at the screen.

I looked down at my card and swallowed hard. "Yes."

Chapter Four

Tiffany

"What is your name?" asked the casting director, a forty-something woman with warm brown eyes.

"Tiffany Banks."

She took off her glasses and began cleaning them with a small green cloth. "Okay, show me what you've got, Tiffany Banks."

I was nervous, so nervous. I opened my mouth to begin, but then froze up.

"Nervous?" she asked, with a small smile.

I smiled weakly. "Yes, I'm sorry."

"Why don't you close your eyes, and try again."

I closed my eyes, inhaled through my nose, and then exhaled slowly.

"Tiffany?"

The song I'd picked out was immediately replaced with the one I couldn't get out of my head. I only hoped that I could do Pink's song justice.

Made a wrong turn, once or twice
Dug my way out, blood and fire
Bad decisions, that's alright
Welcome to my silly life

Mistreated, misplaced, misunderstood
Miss no way, it's all good
It didn't slow me down.

39

Mistaken, always second guessing,
Underestimated, look I'm still around,

Pretty, pretty please,
Don't you ever, ever feel,
Like you're less than, less than
perfect

Pretty, pretty please,
If you ever, ever feel,
Like you're nothing,
You are perfect,
To me.

"Tiffany."

I opened my eyes and stared at the woman, her expression unreadable. I took a deep breath. "So, it was that bad?"

She smiled. "Congratulations, you've made it to the next round."

The back of my eyes began to burn. "Oh...Oh, my God, thank you," I said, blinking back tears. I wanted to jump up and down and scream with joy I was so happy.

"*You* have an amazing voice," she said, handing me back my card. "Now go and show the judges you mean business. One thing, though..."

I leaned forward. "Yes?"

"You'll need to keep your eyes open with them, and keep your chin up. You're exactly the kind of talent we want in the final rounds."

I smiled so broadly that my cheeks hurt. "Okay. Thanks."

She shook my hand, and I walked away, still in shock.

"Oh, my God, you sounded wonderful!" squealed Sinclair, throwing her arms around me. "It actually brought tears to my eyes."

"That *was* pretty amazing," said Jesse. "I'm blown away."

"Thanks," I said, the excitement I'd felt seconds ago was now replaced by terror.

"Okay, what's wrong?" asked Sinclair, staring into my eyes. "You look like you're going to run for the hills."

"What's wrong? I made it."

"Yeah," said Jesse. "Wasn't that the point?"

I bit my lower lip. "I know, but now I have to sing in front of Ransom."

Jesse groaned. "God, you'll be fine. Just do your thing, and don't look at him if you're nervous."

Easy for him to say. I'd been infatuated with Ransom ever since I was eleven years old. The memory of those silvery-blue eyes staring into mine before we kissed still made my knees weak.

"There you go," said Sinclair. "Just ignore him. Chances are he may not even remember you."

"Miss," said one of the staff, a muscular-looking guy wearing a security uniform, and a nametag that said 'Tim'. "You have to move over to the celebrity judges now."

"Okay," I said. "Can my friends come?"

"No, I'm sorry."

"Good luck," said Sinclair, hugging me one last time.

Jesse kissed my cheek. "Break a leg, or whatever."

"Thanks."

I followed Tim to the other side of the field, getting more nervous by the second. By the time we reached the celebrities, and all of cameras, I was shaking.

"Hi," said an older woman with short spiky red hair. She grabbed my card. "I'm Misty; I'm here to prep you. Now, Taylor might do a short interview with you before you're presented to the judges. In fact, looking at you I'm sure he will."

I cleared my throat. "Oh, okay."

She smiled and grabbed my hand. "You poor little thing. Don't be nervous, honey, just do your best, and remember, those celebrities wipe their asses the same way everyone else does, so don't let them intimidate you, especially Tyrone. He can be a little unnerving at times."

I'd watched the show before, and knew he was a hard win. In fact, I was quite sure he'd be the first one to vote "no."

"Now, you understand the rules, you need two out of three judges' votes to get to the next round. Oh, and here," she said, handing me her clipboard. "Read the disclosures, and sign by all the X's. You have approximately five minutes before you will be interviewed by Taylor, and then ushered over to the judges."

"Okay, thanks, Misty."

She patted me on the back. "Good luck, honey."

I skimmed through the disclosures, which were basically the rules of the audition, and signed everything as quickly as possible. As I handed Misty back the clipboard, Taylor approached me with a cameraman.

"Hello," he said, holding out his hand. "Congratulations on making it to this round. I'm Taylor Blake, and you are?"

"Tiffany Banks," I said, placing my hand in his.

His dark eyes regarded me with interest. He squeezed my hand. "What do you know? We have the same first and last letters in our names. Fate has obviously brought us together, young lady. So, Tiffany, would you mind if I interviewed you before you meet the judges?"

I smiled. "Not at all."

"Where are you from?"

"Stanton."

"California girl, nice. What do you do when you're not auditioning for something like this?"

"I'm a hairstylist at *Tangled*, over in Midway City."

He touched his perfectly groomed blonde head and smiled. "Knowing that *Tangled* has such lovely hairdressers, I might have to stop in for a cut very soon."

I blushed. He *was* very good looking, with his puppy-dog eyes and dimples, but not really my type. He was almost *too* perfect looking.

"Well, it would be my pleasure to cut your hair."

"I'll remember that, Tiffany. Now, I guess we'd better start the interview on camera before I get hollered at by the judges," he said, turning to his cameraman. "Roll it."

"Okay," replied the guy.

Taylor moved in closer and put an arm around my shoulders. "Welcome back to 'American Icon', where we have Tiffany Banks waiting to see the judges. Tiffany," he said turning to me. "Let's cut to the chase, do you think you have what it takes to be the next 'American Icon?'"

I forced a smile. "I'm going to give it my best shot."

"Can you sing?"

"I made it this far, so I guess I can hold a tune."

He smiled. "Something tells me you can hold more than a tune. Are you ready to 'wow' the judges, and show them you're not just a pretty face?"

"I'll certainly try."

He squeezed my shoulder. "I have faith in you, Tiffany. Good luck."

"Thanks."

The next thing I knew, I was ushered towards the judges and Ransom, who appeared to be fiddling with his cellphone. My heart beat wildly in my chest as I waited for him to look up and notice me. It was then that I realized that I was still much more nervous about facing him than I was about the audition itself.

Ransom.

I couldn't take my eyes off of him. In fact, I barely recognized him. Stardom had changed Ransom, and I wasn't sure if it was for the better. His dark hair was long, just past his shoulders, and appeared unkempt. He had a goatee, which really needed to be cleaned up, and there were dark circles under his eyes. He looked... haggard.

"Hello, what's your name, honey?" asked Deidra as they handed me a microphone.

I cleared my throat. "It's Tiffany."

Ransom's eyes shot up and locked with mine, sending a wave of heat from my cheeks to the pit of my stomach. One thing that hadn't changed was the effect he still had on me. Ransom had been my first real crush, and even now he could throw my pulse into overdrive just by looking at me.

"What are you going to sing for us today, Tiffany?" asked Tyrone.

I turned to Tyrone. "Hurt, by Christina Aguilera."

Tyrone regarded me shrewdly. "Okay, let's see if you can pull it off."

I closed my eyes, took a deep breath, and then reopened them, focusing on the cameras behind Deidra.

Seems like it was yesterday
When I saw your face,
You told me how proud you were,

But I walked away,
If only I knew what I know today,
Ooh,
Ooh,
I would hold you in my arms,
I would take the pain away,
Thank you for all you've done,
Forgive all your mistakes,
There's nothing I wouldn't do
To hear your voice again,
Sometimes I wanna call you
But I know you won't be there,
Oh, I'm sorry for blaming you,
For everything I just couldn't do,
And I've hurt myself by hurting you,
Some days I feel broke inside
But I won't admit
Sometimes I just wanna hide
'Cause it's you I miss,
And it's so hard to say goodbye
When it comes to this,
ooh,
Would you tell me I was wrong?
Would you help me understand?
Are you looking down upon me?
Are you proud of who I am?
There's nothing I wouldn't do
To have just one more chance,
To look into your eyes
And see you looking back,
Oh, I'm sorry for blaming you,
For everything I just couldn't do,
And I've hurt myself, oh,

"Okay, Tiffany," interrupted Tyrone. "That's good enough."

My palms were sweating as I glanced at Ransom out of the corner of my eye. The look on his face made my stomach clench. He looked... pissed off.

Oh, my God, was I really that bad?

I'd actually thought I'd done pretty well, considering how terrified I was.

Deidra cleared her throat. "Dear, have you had voice lessons?"

"No."

"Have you ever sung in front of strangers?" she asked.

"Um, just my church's congregation," I said. "I was in the choir."

Tyrone smiled and nodded towards the bleachers. "Pardon the pun, but that's a whole different ballgame. You looked like you were ready to run home there for a minute."

I nodded. "I am a little nervous."

"You'll have to work on that, dear," said Deidra. "A performer *needs* to appear confident and ready to take on the world. But fortunately for you, that voice of yours, along with your beautiful, angelic face is distracting enough; the audience might not notice your unease. Anyway, I am definitely giving you a 'Yes'. We need you in this contest. What do you think, Tyrone?"

Tyrone stared at me hard, and then nodded. "Tell you the truth, Tiffany, yours is the best voice I've heard so far. I'm voting 'Yes'. Definitely."

I clasped my hands together, and squealed. "Thank you so much!"

"No problem."

Deidra smiled, and turned to Ransom, who was tapping his fingers on the table rapidly. "What do you think, Ransom?"

"No," he said in that deep, rumbly voice that had made me quiver as a teen.

Deidra's eyebrows shot up. "Are you serious?"

I felt like someone had punched me in the stomach. I blinked back tears.

"No," he said, not meeting my eyes. "Sorry, I vote 'No'. Now, bring on the next contestant."

Chapter Five

Ransom

When I'd first heard Tiffany speak, I'd felt like someone had thrown a bucket of ice-cold water at my face, sobering me up from what was left of my buzz. It had shocked the shit out of me. Little Tiffany Banks, one of my sister's best friends, was actually *here*, trying to get herself onto American Icon.

She had no fucking clue.

It had been years since we'd seen each other. Now she was all grown up, and more beautiful than ever with those wide, blue eyes, cupid lips, and her perky upturned nose. She reminded me of the farmer's daughter, the curvy, gullible one who didn't know how corrupt the world was. Yeah, Tiffany was definitely too naïve and trusting for Hollywood, even *with* that voice, which had taken me by surprise. As amazing as it was, however, there was no way in *hell* I was voting her into this circus of bullshit. Not her. I wouldn't be responsible for that. I'd never forgive myself if my sister's friend ended up like me, a miserable puppet.

"Why in the world did you vote 'No'?" asked Deidra after Tiffany walked away.

"Didn't you see how terrified she was? Hell, she was shitting bricks up there. Face it, that girl will never have *star* presence," I replied. "She's too timid and self-conscious."

"She'll certainly get her shot to prove you wrong," said Tyrone, tapping his pen on the table. "We'll see how she does during the next round, and how the audience and television viewers receive her."

That was the bitch of it. Two out of three votes was all she needed to keep progressing. I'd just need to find a way to get Tyrone or Deidra on my side. Or, to somehow get her ass disqualified.

Tiffany was *not* going to win this contest.

Not on my watch.

***

Tiffany

"He voted *'no'*? You're kidding me," snapped Sinclair, pausing as we walked out of the building. "That egotistical prick! What in the hell is wrong with him?"

I stared down at my shoes. "He must not have thought I had enough talent."

"Let me tell you something, sweetheart," said Jesse, looping his arm through mine as we turned the corner and walked towards the parking lot. "I've heard Ransom sing, and he's not bad, but you... you have more talent than anyone on that show, past *and* present. Hell, I'm still in shock after hearing you sing. I had no idea you were *that* good."

I smiled. "Aw... thanks, Jesse."

"I'm serious. I know talent," he said. "Don't forget... I grew up in Hollywood."

"He did," agreed Sinclair. "And he's right."

"I'm *always* right," he replied with a smirk. "It's a gift."

She rolled her eyes, and then turned to me. "So what's next?"

"I guess I'm headed to Hollywood in a month to meet the competition, and to start performing live. They gave me all the info, I just have to read through everything," I said, holding up the large envelope I'd been given.

"So, are you even more nervous now?" ask Sinclair.

"Actually I'm not too bad, especially now that I've made it through the preliminary auditions."

And facing Ransom.

"Good," said Jesse. "And don't let that judge, Ransom, bring you down. He's obviously an arrogant asshole who thinks he knows it all. You got Tyrone's vote, and that's pretty difficult."

"True," I replied, although I still couldn't believe Ransom had voted "No." When I was a teenager, he'd always teased me and his sister, but had never been downright heartless or cruel. He had to have known how much the audition would mean to me, but apparently didn't seem to give a rat's ass. It was bad enough that the guy I'd fantasized about during high school had not only turned me down when I was a kid, but hadn't thought twice about doing it again.

"So, what about the salon?" asked Sinclair.

"I guess I'll have to take a temporary leave."

"A temporary leave? Are you kidding me, this is the first day of the rest of your life. You're going to be a celebrity, not a service worker any longer," said Jesse. "I'd call them tomorrow and say 'hasta la vista, bitches.'"

Sinclair raised her eyebrows.

He waved his hand. "Oh, you know what I mean," he said. "She should be focusing on preparing for the contest."

"Maybe, but, I would never abandon *Tangled*," I said. "I'm not letting the shop or my clients down. I'm working until the day before I leave. Seriously."

"I still can't believe you're going to be on television," grinned Sinclair, as we slid into Jesse's Jag. "Wait until everyone finds out that you made it to the next round of the competition. They are going to be so proud of you."

I put my seatbelt on and lay my head back against the seat. "You know, it's all so surreal, I'm still trying to absorb everything."

"Absorb this," said Jesse. "You've got talent, oodles of it, and when you win this thing, you can stand on the stage with your chin raised up high, and tell Ransom to go fuck himself."

I smirked. "I might just do it sooner than that."

"Oh, right," said Sinclair. "You're way too nice. You should really start learning how to stand up for yourself. Not let anyone push you around."

"I don't let anyone push me around," I protested.

"Girl, please," said Jesse. "You are *way* too nice. I mean, look at the other day when Felix destroyed your new purse. Most women would have kicked all of the remaining lives out of that mangy cat. But not you. You acted like it was no big deal, but we all obviously knew better. That purse cost you a lot of money and you just brushed it off. Now *that* was being too nice."

"He's a cat," I said. "What should I have done, plotted a deadly revenge?"

"Felix isn't mangy," pouted Sinclair. "He's a handsome little devil."

Jesse's eyes narrowed. "See, even you agree he's evil."

She rolled her eyes. "Gee, and you wonder why he doesn't like you? I guess he can sense your affection."

"Listen, Sin, I like cats but I stopped going near yours right after he bit my hand when I tried petting him the first time, then the second, and finally the third time. He has no love for me, or anyone else."

"He was probably abused as a kitten or something," she protested.

"Right, believe what you want, but let me just say that your cat has some major issues, and probably needs to see my mother's pet therapist. In fact, I'll get that number for you later, Sin."

Sinclair's eyebrows shot up. "Pet therapist?"

"Oh yeah, Ms. Duncan. They call her 'The Cat Whisperer'. She is amazing, she helped mother's cat, Flora, get over her eating disorder."

"Eating disorder?" I asked. "What kind of eating disorder can a cat have?"

He shrugged. "All I know is that she refused to eat for a few days, and then right after Ms. Duncan met with Flora, her appetite came back. Mom raves about her to all of her friends."

"Maybe the cat was just tired of eating the same food?" I asked. "I've heard that even animals get bored sometimes."

"Mimi probably feeds her cat caviar and liver pate," snorted Sinclair. "And that's just on Mondays."

"Believe what you want, but she fixed whatever was wrong with Flora. Anyway," said Jesse. "Back to the subject at hand – Tiffany you really do need to stop taking shit from people. If you don't, you'll definitely never make it in Hollywood. My dad would tell you that."

Jesse's dad was a casting director who'd recently retired. From what Sinclair had told me, he was a real tool who thought he was some kind of Hollywood Godfather or something ridiculous like that. She couldn't stand the man.

"How *is* dear old dad?" asked Sinclair, with a look of distaste. "Is he still living with that young actress?"

He frowned. "Yes, that bimbo is going through his money like water, too. He just bought her a new Astin Martin along with tickets to Italy for next week. It makes me sick how she uses him.”

“I’m sure he uses her, too, so they’re obviously made for each other,” replied Sinclair.

My cellphone began to ring. I pulled it out of my purse and looked at the number, but didn’t recognize it. “Hello?”

“Oh, my God, Tiff?! It’s Remy!”

I grinned. “Remy! How are you, it’s been so long!”

I hadn’t seen Remy since we’d graduated high school, and she’d left for T.C.U. while I’d stayed back in Stanton to go to beauty school. We’d tried keeping in touch, but eventually lost track of each other.

“I’m doing okay. I heard you’re a finalist on American Icon! I can’t believe it. Well, actually I can, you always had a kick-ass voice.”

“Thanks,” I said. “So, what are you up to these days?”

“I’m engaged, and working in New York right now.”

“You’re engaged! Seriously?”

Like me, she was only twenty-one, but it didn’t surprise me that she was engaged. She was beautiful, just like her brother, and people were drawn to her outgoing personality.

“Yes, you’ve met him, in fact,” she said, with a hint of laughter.

“Who?”

“Taylor Blake.”

“Shut up, seriously?”

"Yes. We're getting married next month. In fact, I'm holding your invitation right now. I just didn't know how to get ahold of you. Your phone number is obviously unlisted, and now that your mother's gone…"

"Yeah, I know," I answered softly. "I'm kind of unreachable."

She sighed. "I'm so sorry about your mother, Tiff. She was such a sweetheart."

"She was," I said, smiling sadly. "I still can't believe she's not here."

"I um… I'm sorry I didn't make the funeral. When I heard about it, I was in the middle of a nervous breakdown, I don't know if you heard about it. I just didn't think I could handle seeing her laid to rest. I spent so much time at your house growing up. Shit," she choked. "I feel so horrible about not being there for you, Tiff. I should have been stronger."

"It's okay," I murmured. "And yes, I heard what happened from your mother."

Remy had been dating someone in college who'd committed suicide. It had happened right before my mother had died.

"Still, I wish I would have done things differently. I hope you can forgive me."

"Don't worry about it, Rem. You had your own problems to deal with. It was a bad year for everyone. Anyway, how are you doing *now*?" I asked, feeling sad that I hadn't been able to be there for her either. We'd always been so close growing up.

"I'm doing great, actually. And my fiancé, he's wonderful," she said. "We're really in love."

I smiled. It was good to hear. "I'm very happy for you."

"And I'm so proud of you, Tiff, for auditioning."

"So, how did you find out? Ransom?"

"Yes, he found your phone number and then sent me a message."

"That's what I figured."

She sighed. "That's another reason why I'm calling. He asked me to talk to you, although when he told me why, I almost told him to fuck off."

"I don't understand," I said.

She paused. "Ransom wants you to drop out of the contest."

Chapter Six

Tiffany

"For real?" asked Felicia, staring at me from across the salon, her eyes wide.

It was the day after my audition, and we were the only people in the salon, save for our two customers seated before us.

"Yup, *and* he had his sister call me. He asked her to try and talk me out of continuing with the contest."

She put a hand on her waist. "Did you tell them both to kiss your fucking ass?"

I glanced towards her customer, expecting a look of disapproval on her elderly face, but instead, she stared back at me with a straight face, and said, "Fucking-snot-boogers."

It was then that I remembered, it was old Mrs. Conway who has Tourette's Syndrome.

Trying not to laugh, I replied, "Not in those exact words," I said, raising my customer's chair. "But basically, yes."

"Good, because if you would have agreed, I would have had to slap you silly."

"And I'd deserve it."

"So, why does he want you to drop out?"

"I'm not really sure. Maybe he thinks I suck."

"You don't suck. You have a great voice. Obviously, Tyrone and that other judge thought so too," replied Felicia.

I sighed. "Still, he voted 'No'."

She waved her hand. "He's obviously a real idiot."

"Maybe, but there has to be a reason why he wants me to drop out. Maybe it's because we know each other, and *he's* afraid of getting kicked off the show?"

"Past tense. You *knew* each other."

"Still, I just can't believe he asked Remy to work on me."

"You actually *know* Ransom?" asked the seventeen-year-old girl in my chair. I thought she'd been too involved with the magazine she was reading, until I saw a picture of Ransom on the page in front of her. Another young fan.

"Not really. I mean, I knew him before he was famous."

She sighed dreamily. "Is he as gorgeous in real life as he is on television?"

"Cock-bite-shithead," murmured Mrs. Conway.

Smiling, I turned back to my customer. "Well..."

Just then the front door of the salon jingled, letting us know that someone had entered. I stepped around the partition to see who it was, and nearly dropped my comb.

Ransom.

Along with two men, who I assumed were *his* bodyguards, although, at six-foot-four, he towered over the both of them.

Taking a deep breath, I set the comb down on the counter. "Excuse me. I'll be back in a minute, Eve."

"Okay."

Ransom stared at me with such intensity as I moved towards him, that I was suddenly conscious of every step I took.

Nobody had a right to look that handsome, I thought. The fact that he was dressed in a tight, white T-shirt with low-riding jeans, and had obviously spent *some* kind of time in the gym didn't help matters either.

"Ransom," I said. "What an unexpected surprise."

One corner of his mouth twitched. "You left out 'pleasant'."

I smiled coolly. "Did I?"

He let out a low, rumbly chuckle and something whirled in my stomach.

I folded my arms under my chest. "What do you want?"

He looked around. "This is a salon, right? Isn't it obvious?" he said, running a hand through his long hair. "I need a haircut."

"I see that. Let me check when Felicia is available," I said, grabbing the schedule. There was no way in hell I was going to cut his hair.

He stepped closer to the counter and leaned forward. "Are you available?" he asked in a low voice. "Because you're the only one I want touching me."

I knew what he meant but it didn't stop my cheeks from burning. I stared down at the schedule, petrified of looking up into those silvery eyes. "I'm busy right now," I replied softly. "If you

can come back in an hour, I might be able to fit
you in."

He tapped his fingers on the counter.
"That's fine, my afternoon is free. I'll just wait
here."

Crap.

"Uh, are you sure? There's a coffee shop
next door, maybe you'd like to wait over there
instead?" I asked, looking up. "It might be
awhile."

He cocked an eyebrow. "Ms. Banks, are
you trying to get rid of me?"

"Isn't it the other way around?" I said
quickly, unable to stop myself.

Our eyes held for a few seconds, and then
he grinned. "Touché."

I pointed towards a stack of magazines
sitting on the coffee table over in the lounge.
"Well, if you are going to stay, there are some
magazines to keep you busy. We also have a soda
machine in back, if you need caffeine or sugar."

He nodded, and ran a hand through his
wavy dark hair. "Thanks."

"You bet."

He turned back towards his security
guards, murmured something, and seconds later
they left the salon without him.

I put down the pen and nodded. "Um, I'll
be back at my station if you need anything."

"I'll be fine," he said, walking over towards
the magazines. He picked up one of the tabloids
and snorted. "Looks like I made the cover again.
Oh, and look, I'm a father of triplets."

My eyes widened. "Triplets?"

He walked over to the garbage can, and threw the magazine away. "Fuck! The bullshit they come up with."

"So, it's not true?"

His eyebrows lifted. "You're kidding me, right?"

"My friend told me that there is usually some truth about all of those stories," I replied stiffly. I didn't like the way he was looking at me. As if I was gullible.

"The only thing true about that particular magazine is the month and year on the cover. Don't believe everything you hear or see."

"So in other words, you're not an out-of-control rock star who drinks too much, drives like a bat out of hell, and gets tested monthly for AIDS?"

"Rolling Stone *may* have exaggerated a little. I always use a condom, and don't need to be tested for AIDS nearly that much. I also don't drive when I'm trashed. At least not that I can remember."

"They had you all wrong, then," I replied with a smirk.

He grinned and then picked up a magazine with a sexy model on the front. "Looks like Sela Royce is pregnant."

"Do you know her?" I asked, remembering that Sela had once been engaged to Sinclair's boyfriend.

"I only knew her one night," he said, grinning wickedly. "At least, that's what *she* said.

I guess I was too shitfaced to recall much of
anything."

I shook my head. "You're really messed up,
you know that?"

He raised his eyebrows. "Hey, she's the one
who took advantage of me when I was hammered.
You tell me who's more messed up?"

I rolled my eyes.

"It's tough being me," he went on, sitting
down near the window. "Women are always trying
to take advantage of me. I mean, hell, God not
only gave me a decent voice, but he also made me
irresistible. It's damn exhausting."

"Same old Ransom, I see. Cocky and
arrogant."

"I wish I was the same old Ransom," he
answered, his face growing serious. He opened up
the magazine, and started flipping through it. "So,
I guess I'll be right here when you're ready for
me."

"Okay," I said, wondering if he was
breaking some kind of 'American Icon' rule by
being here, and if so, why he was risking it. I
knew one thing; there was no way in hell I'd let
him talk me out of dropping out of the contest. I
didn't know what kind of game he was playing,
but I wasn't the young girl he once knew, nor was
I easily manipulated.

Chapter Seven

Ransom

I stretched my legs out and yawned as I caught glimpses of Tiffany while she cut her client's hair. I'd been up most of the night again, this time sober, which was rare. But, I needed to clear my head and figure out how I was going to persuade her to drop out of the competition.

Taffy.

Seeing her today only strengthened my resolve. She was still naïve and much too innocent for Hollywood. I'd witnessed firsthand how tainted the road to superstardom could be, and if she went all the way, I was convinced that, like me, she'd lose herself, and regret making the wrong choices for the rest of her life.

Our eyes met briefly again as she peeked around the partition, and I bit back a smile. From the way she'd blushed, it was obvious that she still had a little crush on me, just like when she was a teenager. But she wasn't in junior high anymore, and the young, doe-eyed girl I remembered had grown into a beautiful, sexy young woman. One I had to remember, was off limits.

But *damn* had she blossomed.

It didn't help that today she wore a short, yellow sundress that emphasized her toned legs, and delicate tanned shoulders. The horny bastard that I was, pictured her thighs wrapped around

She raised her hand, and I stared in awe at her long, blue nails, wondering how anyone could cut hair with those talons. "Whatever, just listen up, okay? I don't know what kind of game you're playin', but my girl, Tiffany, she can sing. With a voice like that, she don't need to be cutting hair, or any of this shit, so quit doing whatever it is that you're doing, and let her be, you know what I'm saying?"

I cocked an eyebrow. "Whatever it is that I'm doing?"

She glared at me. "Don't play me, Mr. rock star, okay? I'm not twenty-one, and I'm not wet behind the ears. Stay out of Tiffany's way in this contest. You got yours, and now it's her turn to get hers."

"But –"

"Na... na... na... " she said, wagging her index finger. "No buts. Just let the girl reach for her own stars, and keep your ass planted on the ground, far away from her. You feel me?"

"Ah... I guess."

She pursed her lips, and glared at me. "You guess? Let me tell you something –"

"Hey, what's going on over here?" asked Tiffany, coming up behind the other stylist.

"It's all good, I'm just welcoming Mr. Celebrity into our salon, Tiff," said the woman, turning away. She walked back to her customer, hips swaying with attitude. "Make sure he understands a few things."

Tiffany raised her eyebrows.

I shrugged.

"Could you do me a favor?" asked Tiffany.

"What?"

"My customer, Eve, wants your autograph, but she's too shy to ask you herself."

I looked over at the young girl peeking around the room divider, and winked at her, making her giggle. "Of course."

Tiffany handed me a notepad and pen. "Thanks, Ransom."

When I finished writing, I handed the notepad back to Tiffany, and she read it. "To Eve, dream big, and never lose sight of yourself. Ransom," she smiled. "Oh, that's very sweet."

"Yep, that's me. Sweet," I replied dryly.

She chuckled. "So, I'm almost done with Eve. You still doing okay?"

I cracked a smile and stretched my arms behind my head. "Don't worry about me. I'm doing just fine here."

I was actually doing better than fine. For the first time in a while, I was doing something completely normal – waiting to get my hair cut without bodyguards or media annoying the fuck out of me.

"Well, good."

"Just take your time," I said, closing my eyes. "I don't mind waiting."

Chapter Eight

Tiffany

"So," I said when Ransom planted his butt into my chair ten minutes later. "How do you want it?"

He raised his eyebrows, and stared at me in the mirror. "How can I get it?" he asked with a wicked grin.

I groaned. "For thirty dollars, not the way you're thinking."

He laughed, and I couldn't help but crack a smile of my own as I draped the plastic cape around his shoulders.

"How long have you been doing this?"

"About two years," I replied, noticing that my hands were trembling slightly. The affect he had on me was unnerving.

"Do you like it?"

"I really do. It's fun improving people's images."

He rubbed his chin. "Hm..."

"Seriously," I said, running my fingers through his hair, enjoying it more than I probably should. "What do you want?"

"Hell, just cut it all off," he said, waving his hand. "Well... not all of it... just make it short. I need a change."

"Okay, if you say so," I said. "Why don't you follow me, and we'll wet your hair down?"

He stood up, followed me over to the sink, and then sat down on the brown leather reclining chair.

"Lean back, please," I said, turning on the water.

He did, and then looked up at me, his eyes studying my face intently.

"What?" I asked, suddenly feeling very self-conscious.

His lips curled up. "Nothing."

"You know, you *can* close your eyes."

"Does my staring bother you? Hell, most girls would be thrilled," he said with a shit-eating grin.

"I'm not *most* girls. Besides, we've known each other for years, and I'm not going to fawn over you just because you're famous now."

"No?"

I grabbed the hose and began rinsing his hair with warm water. "No. Now, close your eyes."

He closed his eyes, and smirked. "I never knew you were so damn bossy, Taffy."

I deliberately sprayed his eyelids with water.

He frowned.

"Oh, sorry," I said innocently

He wiped the water from his eyelid with his fingertips, and pursed his lips. "Right."

"So, um, is the water temperature okay? Not too hot or cold?" I asked, staring at his lips, remembering how I'd been there before.

Crap, why did I still have to be so attracted to this man?

Even now I pictured myself sitting on his lap in the damn recliner, straddling him. I'd be lying if I said that watching him perform onstage hadn't made me all hot and bothered, along with most of his other female fans. Now he was here, in my shop, and I still wanted to jump his bones.

His grin was dark and sexy. "It's pretty good but if you want to go hotter, damn girl, I won't object one bit."

I swallowed. "Hotter?"

"Yeah, think you can handle that?" he teased, sending a wave of heat directly to my pelvis.

"Actually, I think we'd better cool you down," I replied in a husky voice. Obviously I was the one who needed to be cooled down.

He opened his eyes and grabbed my wrist to stop me from adjusting the water. "Hey, I'm not ready to be cooled down. Now, unless you're prepared to get wet *with* me," he said in that deep, silky voice of his, "I'm going to request that you keep that water the way it is, and no funny business."

"I'll leave it alone," I replied, feeling the heat rise into my cheeks. I wasn't sure which was crazier, the fact that we were arguing about the water or how excited it was making me.

He released my wrist and closed his eyes, again. "Too bad. I kind of liked the idea of seeing you wet."

Oh, hell, if I wasn't wet already...

Needing to compose myself, I shoved all kinky thoughts of him out of my mind, and changed the subject. "So, um, what's it like being famous?"

His lips tightened. "Not nearly as thrilling as you think."

"Oh, why is that?"

Before he could answer, Felicia peeked her head around the corner. "Tiffany, Justin is here."

My stomach turned sour. "What?"

Her eyes narrowed. "Yeah, you want me to get rid of him?"

That was one thing I loved about Felicia, she wasn't afraid to bust anyone's balls.

I sighed. "No, I'll just see what he wants."

Justin was my ex-boyfriend – my slightly psychotic ex-boyfriend – who had a temper and a jealous streak that had snuck up on me right after I'd turned twenty-one, and had become of legal age to drink. We'd been dating for two months, and he'd actually been an amazingly attentive boyfriend until my very first 'girl's-night-out', where he ended up showing his true colors. I still felt nauseated as I thought back to that night, which had started out awesome but ended so horribly.

"You went clubbing in that?" he'd asked after my friends had dropped me off at my apartment, where I found him sitting alone in the dark, obviously waiting for me.

I'd stared down at my faded blue jeans, white camisole, and mini jean jacket, wondering what had gotten him so riled up. All of my skin had been covered, save for a little cleavage, but that was only when I'd bent down. In fact, most of the girls in the bar had been naked compared to what I'd been wearing that night. "What's wrong with my clothes?"

He'd chugged down the rest of his beer, and set it on the glass coffee table. "Your jeans are too tight, and everyone in the club was probably leering at your tits, which are barely covered in that little top," he'd slurred. "It's not really appropriate, unless you're trying to draw attention to yourself."

Shocked at his behavior, I'd laughed nervously. "Justin, there's nothing wrong with this outfit. You know that I dress like this all the time at work. Besides, if someone had been checking me out, who really cares? You're my boyfriend, and the only one that matters."

He'd stood up, swaying slightly. "That's right, you're *my* girl. So why are you going out advertising something that belongs to me, unless," his eyes had hardened, "it's still up for grabs?"

I'd stared at him in shock. "That's totally unfair. What is *wrong* with you? Why are you getting so bent out of shape over my clothes?"

He'd lunged towards me and grabbed both of my forearms, squeezing them painfully. "Look," he'd growled, his fingers digging into my skin, "from now on, you're not going out with any of these so-called 'friends' unless *I'm* invited, too."

I'd shoved him away and took a step back. "What the hell is wrong with you?!"

He'd stared at me for a minute, rigid and ready to explode. But then, as if someone had pulled a switch, he'd smiled and turned on the syrupy charm that had made me fall for him in the first place.

"God, I'm sorry, babe," he'd said, his brown eyes softening. "I guess I've just had a little too much to drink tonight. If you want to dump my ass for being a total prick, I'd totally understand."

Obviously, he'd been drunk. "No, just don't ever grab me like that again or act so crazy," I'd said, feeling a little dizzy from drinking. "Wow, I really don't feel so good."

"Come on, babe," he'd said, putting his arm around my shoulders and guiding me towards the bedroom. "Let's just go to bed. It's late."

Tired, dizzy, and still tipsy from all of the shots my girlfriends had given me, I'd agreed. Unfortunately, that's when things turned even uglier.

"I can't... I don't feel very well," I'd mumbled after we'd gotten under the sheets, and his hand had moved between my legs.

He'd tensed up. "Excuse me?"

"Justin," I'd pleaded, feeling queasy. "I drank too much, and I don't feel good... I just can't do this right now."

"Not in the mood, huh? Why, did you *already* fuck someone else tonight?"

I'd stared at him in horror. "What?"

"I bet you're still thinking about the guy right now, aren't you?"

Groaning, I'd rolled away from him. "You're talking crazy..."

"You're *mine*," he'd growled, grabbing my arm, "and I'm going to make sure you don't *ever* forget it." Then, he'd forced himself on me while I lay there, sobbing underneath his hard, cruel thrusts. When it was over, he'd said nothing, just rolled over, and passed out into a drunken stupor. The next morning, he'd tried to apologize, but it had forever changed the way I'd viewed him. There was no way I'd wanted someone like that in my life. I'd told him to leave, and then spent the next month trying to avoid his calls, his flowers, and his excuses. Eventually, he'd given up harassing me, and I'd heard that he'd starting dating someone else.

"Okay," I said, turning to Ransom. "I'll get you back to my station, and then I'm going to find out what's going on."

He stood up, and stared down into my eyes. "So, who's Justin?"

"Just this guy I dated a little while back."

"You don't sound very happy to hear from him."

I shrugged. "I guess you could say that our relationship didn't end well."

His face darkened. "Does he need to be reminded that you're not together anymore? I'd be happy to set him straight, if you'd like."

The look on his face was totally serious, and I couldn't help but smile. "No, but thanks."

"If you need any interference from me, just say the word."

"Right," I said, as he followed me back to my chair. "You get into a fight and the media finds out…"

"Screw the media," he answered, sitting down.

"Ransom, I'm pretty sure that you shouldn't even be here. You have much more to lose than I do."

He looked in the mirror and ran a hand through his damp hair. "So, let them fire me. I really don't give a shit."

"Seriously?"

Our eyes met. "Hell, being a judge on this show wasn't even my idea. My manager set it up, thinking it would be good for my career."

I raised my eyebrows. "Why, is it in trouble?"

He shrugged. "Doesn't seem that way. I'm selling plenty of records, I've got a tour set up, and the money is rolling in faster than I can spend it. As far as I'm concerned, the only thing dying in my career is my interest."

"How could you even say that? Isn't this what you've always wanted? Fame and fortune? Platinum records?"

"Taffy, this gig isn't all it's cracked up to be. Especially when you're dealing with 'American Icon'. You win on that show, and you ultimately lose, because when it's all said and done, they *own* your ass. Hell, I'm locked in with them for the next few years."

I stared at him incredulously. "Sorry, but forgive me if I'm not playing a violin solo for you.

Most artists would give their souls for what you have."

"I already did, and let me tell you, it wasn't worth it."

"Pussy-whining-wiener-head," belted out Mrs. Conway from across the room, as Felicia teased her hair.

I bit my lip, and Felicia turned her head away, trying to control her laughter.

Ransom cocked his eyebrow, and turned towards the old woman, who stared back at us with a straight face.

I bent down, and whispered. "Tourette's Syndrome"

"Likely excuse," he grinned.

"I'll be right back," I said. "Try to ignore her. She can't help it, and gets embarrassed if you comment about it."

"She didn't look too embarrassed when she called me a pussy-whining-wiener-head," he chuckled.

I glanced at her as I walked towards the front of the salon, and from the satisfied look on her face, I had to agree.

"Tiffany," said Justin, as I approached him. I had to admit, asshole or not, he was still handsome with his windswept styled hair, and deep brown eyes.

I forced a smile. "Hi, Justin. Are you here for a trim?"

"No," he said. "I just wanted to stop by personally and congratulate you on getting into American Icon."

I pushed my hair behind my ears. "Oh, you heard about that?"

He nodded. "Yeah. I ran into Jesse at Geno's, and he mentioned it."

Geno's was a pizza place a few blocks away.

"Thanks," I said, glancing towards the clock, wishing he'd take the hint that I wasn't in the mood for talking, and would just leave.

"Listen," he said, lowering his voice. "We need to talk."

"About what?"

He sighed. "I... I miss what we had. Don't you?"

I only missed the man I thought he was, not the paranoid lunatic who basically raped me. "Look," I said. "I'm really busy right now. It's not a good time."

"How about we have dinner at that restaurant you used to love, El Sinada?"

"Justin, I really can't," I said. "And if you want to know the truth, I think it would better if you just forgot about me and moved on with your life."

He stepped closer and lowered his voice. "Listen, I've changed. In fact, that's kind of why I wanted to talk to you. I'm not using anymore."

I stared at him in surprise. "Not *using*? Using what?"

"I never told you," he said, his face reddening. "But, I um, I had a little problem with cocaine."

It was definitely news to me but somehow, it made a lot of sense. Even before the night he'd freaked out, he'd seemed a little too hyper and edgy.

"Cocaine? Really? I had no idea."

He smiled, sheepishly. "Yeah. I guess it made me a little paranoid and kind of crazy at times."

I crossed my arms under my chest. "Congratulations on kicking it. You should be proud of yourself. I mean it."

He nodded. "Yeah, I am pretty proud. I haven't used in six weeks, and I'm getting my shit together."

"I'm very happy for you," I said. "And I mean that... but," I lowered my voice, "even so, it's over between us, Justin. We can be friends, but seriously, that's it."

His faced darkened. "Just friends? You're really not going to give me a second chance?"

"I'm sorry, really I am. I've moved on, though, and so should you."

"Everything okay over here?" interrupted Ransom, approaching from behind me.

"This isn't any of your business, pal," said Justin, staring up at Ransom. "So just walk away."

He smiled coldly. "At the moment, it *is* my business. You're bothering my stylist, and she was just about to trim my hair. The idea of her cutting it while she's upset doesn't sound like it's going to be in my best interest."

Justin's eyes narrowed. "You look familiar. Do I know you?"

He crossed his arms under his chest. "Yeah, I'm the guy you don't want to piss off. Now, do us all a favor and get lost before things escalate into something that I promise, *pal*, won't go the way you're planning."

"You're actually threatening me?"

"I'm just giving you some friendly advice. I think you've overstayed your welcome, by a long shot."

"Fuck you," snapped Justin, his fists clenched. Obviously he'd kicked the drugs but not his temper tantrums.

Ransom took a step forward. "I'll take that as you need a little more persuading."

"I'd like to see you try, asshole."

"Enough," I said, stepping between them. I turned to Justin, whose face was still red. "Please, Justin, just leave."

He pointed towards Ransom. "Tell this fucker to get out of my face first."

Sighing, I turned to Ransom. "Please, just let it go. I'm fine. Really."

Ransom remained silent but I could tell he was still waiting for Justin to make a move.

"Please," I murmured, grasping his upper arm, which was hard and tense.

Just then, two young customers entered the store, staring at the three of us curiously.

"Hello," I said, removing my hand from Ransom's bicep. "Can I help you guys?"

"Supposed to get a trim," said the dark-haired teen, pushing his bangs out of his eyes.

"Hey," said the other boy with blonde hair, to Ransom.

He smiled at the two young men who looked like they'd rather be hitting the waves than getting their hair trimmed. "Hey, what's up?"

Recognition lit up the blonde surfer guy's eyes. "Are you...?"

"No. But I get that all the time," he interrupted quickly. He then turned to me, his eyes twinkling. "Listen, babe, I'll go sit down. Don't be too long, you know we have a lot of things to do before our dinner reservation, later." Then he bent down and planted a quick kiss on my lips, stunning the hell out of me.

"Uh, okay," I answered breathlessly. How many times had I lay in bed as a teenager, dreaming of the day that Ransom would do something like that? On his own accord? Obviously he was putting on a show, but it still gave me goose bumps.

"Don't be long," he said, slapping my rear.

I touched my backside, and stared at him in shock.

He winked, and then walked back towards my station.

Still stunned, I glanced at Justin, who was visibly seething. When our eyes met, his were filled with accusation and betrayal.

I smiled weakly, and then turned towards the two boys. "Give me a second, and I'll check the schedule, see if we can fit you in. We're a little short-staffed today."

"No problem," said the dark-haired teen, pulling out his cellphone, and sitting down in the chair next to his buddy, who was already busy texting someone.

"Seriously? You're with that dickhead?" whispered Justin.

"I'm sorry, but you knew it was over between us."

Shaking his head, he turned on his heel, and stormed out of the salon.

"What in the hell was that all about?" asked Felicia, coming up behind me as I pulled out the schedule.

I cleared my throat. "Ransom got rid of Justin for me."

"I saw that," she answered with a small smile. "*And* heard about it. Girl, old Mrs. Conway had my ears burning when she caught a glimpse of you two locking lips. That old woman knows more cuss words than my nephew, Wylie, and he's from Detroit."

"Oh, God," I giggled.

"Mm... hmm..."

"So, can you take one of these guys?" I asked, motioning towards them.

She glanced down at the schedule, and nodded. "Sure, I've got room for one more. Then I have to head out, Devon is taking me bowling tonight."

Devon was her newest boyfriend, and a real sweetheart. He owned his a bar and had twin daughters who helped him run it. I'd never seen Felicia so happy.

"Bowling?" I laughed, looking at her long nails. "How are you going to manage that?"

She put a hand on her waist. "Honey, I'm not bowling. Devon's on a team, and I'm just going to root for him while I kick back, and enjoy some much needed margaritas."

I smiled. "Now that sounds nice."

"Why don't you join us?"

I nodded towards the clock. "I wish I could, but I have an early appointment tomorrow with Mrs. Hauglish. I need all the sleep I can get to deal with that woman."

"That old battle-ax who bitches and moans the entire time you're doing her hair?"

"The one and only."

"Girl, you've got the patience of a saint. The first time I heard her snapping at you, I had to hold my tongue, and you know how hard that is."

I laughed. "Yeah, she's difficult but her tips are outrageous. I just take everything she says with a grain of salt."

"If you win 'Icon', you won't have to deal with women like that anymore."

"Very true, although I'd miss all of my coworkers," I said, hip-checking her.

She smiled. "We'd miss you, too."

Just then, Ransom's two security guards stepped back into the salon.

"Oh, I'd better finish him up," I said as the two guys eyed me curiously.

She grabbed a pen. "You do that, and I'll schedule these two boys in."

"Thanks."

Chapter Nine

Ransom

"I was wondering if I had to come back out there and throw his ass out the front door," I told Tiffany when she returned, and re-clipped the brown plastic cape around my neck. She picked up her comb and scissors, and the fruity scent of her perfume, along with the proximity of her tits near my face, made it difficult to sit comfortably.

"Sorry," she said, looking slightly distracted. She stepped behind me, and our eyes met in the mirror. "So, you wanted it short, right? How short are you thinking on the top?"

"Surprise me."

She looked at my chin. "Okay. I'll clean up your goatee, if you'd like, too."

I rubbed my hand over it, and nodded. "Sounds good."

"So," I said, after a few minutes of silent trimming, "you going to comment about that kiss?"

She chuckled. "Actually, I don't know who was more surprised, me or Justin."

"Hopefully that asshole will leave you alone now."

Her lip twitched. "Now, how do you know he's an asshole?"

"Because anyone who lets a girl like you go must have screwed up, big time."

Her cheeks turned pink. "Thanks, Ransom. Turns out he was an asshole, but it was because he was using cocaine during that time. He just told me."

"Cocaine alone won't make someone an asshole, but you're obviously too good for that dirt-bag."

Our eyes met in the mirror. "What about you?"

I raised my eyebrows. "What do you mean?"

She moved in front of me, and started trimming my bangs. "Is it true what they say, that you're into some hard stuff?"

I stole another glance at her chest, which was right in my face and thought that the only thing hard at the moment was my dick. "This isn't about me," I said, pulling my eyes away from her cleavage. "It's about your ex, and why you should stay away from guys like him."

"You're preaching to the choir," she said. "I'm not interested in going back with that guy. Not after..."

"Not after what?"

She shrugged. "Just... I'm not going back with him, no matter what. I'm not interested in going down that road again."

"Good because his road appears to be a dead end. So," I grinned. "Where do you want to eat tonight?"

She stopped cutting. "Are you asking me out?"

"Just to make it look legit, you know? In case he's waiting for you when you get off of work."

"You seriously don't care about getting kicked off the show? I mean, it's not like we can go anywhere together in public. It would be bad for both of us. Speaking of which," her eyes narrowed. "Thanks for voting 'No', by the way."

I was wondering when she was going to bring that up. "Look, I had a very good reason to vote that way. If you go out to dinner with me tonight, I'll even tell you why."

"Why can't you just do it now, and save yourself some money?"

"Money obviously isn't a concern. Just have dinner with me."

She sighed. "Are you sure you're not trying to get me kicked off of the show?"

"No," I said, although there was always that route to consider. It was lowdown and devious, but an interesting thought.

"Good answer, especially since I'm holding the scissors. I don't know about dinner, though. If you ask me, it's too risky."

I smiled innocently. "Oh, come on. Nobody will recognize me with my hair buzzed."

"I really don't know if I want to take that chance," she replied. "You're practically a name brand, Ransom. Everyone knows your face."

"Come on. I know of this little hole in the wall that's discreet, and serves *the* best burgers in the world. Swear to God. Let me buy you one, and we'll catch up on old times."

"A hole in the wall, huh? Where's this place?"

"It's called Jimbo's, in Santa Ana. It's a real dive, but their burgers are killer and if you like southwestern food, the guacamole is excellent."

She grabbed an electric clipper, and began trimming the sides of my hair. "Okay. What about your security guys? Are they going to be joining us?"

"Fuck no. We'll ditch them. You've got a back door in this place, right?"

Her eyes widened. "Can't you just tell them to go home?"

"No. I'm not the one who signs their paychecks. They belong to American Icon and they pretty much demand round-the-clock security on me. It's a real pain in the ass."

"Maybe we should just forget it. I don't want you to get into trouble."

I grinned. "You realize who you're talking to, right?"

She laughed. "I suppose it would be odd if you stayed out of trouble, wouldn't it?"

"Damn right, so don't try and change me, woman."

"Well," she said stepping back. She folded her arms under her chest. "Looks like it's too late."

I turned towards the mirror, and nodded my approval. She'd trimmed the sides short and left it a little longer on top. If I got rid of the five-o'clock shadow, I'd probably looked more like a stockbroker than the rocker who'd walked in earlier. I ran my fingers through the top of my hair, and smirked. "Damn and I didn't think I could get any better looking."

She snorted. "You're such a goon."

She sprayed something into the top of my hair, and raked her hands through it. "This is a texturizing spray. It gives your hair a little more dimension."

"Are you saying that I should buy this?" I asked, as she handed me the bottle.

"Only if you want to keep your hair looking this way."

I cocked my head to the side. "What if I hired you as my personal stylist? Then you could make sure my hair looks this way every day."

"I'm surprised you don't have a personal stylist already."

I grinned wickedly. "I do but I much prefer your hands touching me instead of his."

"Well, thanks for the offer but obviously that's not even remotely feasible."

"Why not?" I asked, the idea sounding better by the moment. "Seriously, I'd pay you triple of what you're making here. Hell, I'll even double that offer if you'd be willing to come to Europe with me when I tour."

"Obviously that's very tempting. But Ransom, obviously you know that I'm involved with the show right now."

"Yeah, and so am I. But Taffy, there is life after American Icon. Don't forget that."

"I know," she sighed. "My chances are probably pretty slim of winning the competition anyway."

"I'm not going to lie; the competition you're performing against is stiff. There are some really talented artists you're competing against."

She studied my face for a minute, and then raised her chin. "Ransom, tell me the truth – you don't think I have what it takes to win, do you? That's why you voted 'No', isn't it?"

It was obvious that she thought I didn't think so, and the wounded look on her heart-shaped face was wrecking me. Fuck, I hated being an asshole, but, it was for her own good. "It's not that you're a *bad* singer," I replied, choosing my words carefully. The fact was that her voice had taken me by surprise. It was strong and very sexy. There was no way I'd tell her that, however. At least not until the competition was over. If she was still interested in being a singer, I'd have her back, and help her make the right decisions. Until then, I'd have to lie through my teeth. "You're better than most. But this is American Icon. The best of the best. Not only do you have to sing like an angel, but you need the confidence and the stage presence to pull it all off."

"So, what are you trying to say?" she asked, her eyes filling with tears.

I groaned inwardly.

Fuck.

"Just... think about my offer. Hell, more money and the chance to travel Europe? Come on, Taffy."

She turned away, and I could tell that she was brushing at tears. Her sensitivity confirmed that I was right – she didn't have a hard enough shell for this business.

"Taff?"

"I'll definitely think about it," she answered softly. "I mean, I'd be stupid to refuse the money, and," she turned back around, and managed a smile, "who wouldn't want to travel around the world with a legendary rock star?"

"Legendary? I don't know about that." I stood up, and moved closer. "Listen, I'm sorry," I said, hugging her. "You're a sweet kid," I murmured into her hair, which smelled like honey and vanilla. "Just don't get your hopes up too high for winning this thing. It's just a show, and doesn't have to be the defining factor in your life. Hell, if I were you, I'd just drop out now, and save yourself a lot of heartache later."

She suddenly went rigid, and then pulled away. "Well, you're not me, and I'm not one to give up that easily. Besides, you won the competition, and now you're living larger than life. Is it so wrong that I want to see where this thing takes *me*?"

"It's only wrong if you can't face the end results without feeling like you failed the contest. This is going to be a stressful ride. You're going to get criticized by everyone, the other contestants are going to start getting nasty, and the world is going to be judging you. I'm just trying to save you a lot of mental anguish."

"I'm a big girl now, Ransom. I appreciate your advice, but I've got to try, and if I don't win, so be it. But I'm not going to just quit that easily."

"But why even put yourself through –"

"I'm not finished," she interrupted, her jaw set. "I know that you don't want me in this contest, I'm not stupid, so don't bother trying to talk me out of it. In fact," she said, grabbing a broom, "my mom didn't raise a quitter. If she was here right now, she'd tell me to keep my chin up, and not let anyone stand in my way. Including you."

I had to admire her stubbornness. "Your mom was a strong and thoughtful woman. I didn't know her very well, but she obviously raised her daughter the same way."

She smiled proudly. "Damn right. You know, she once told me that it's not always about winning, but facing the challenges head-on with a smile, no matter how terrified you are."

"Sounds like she may have had to follow her own advice," I said softly.

"She did and that's why I have to do this. For her as well as myself."

"I get that."

"Good. So, you're seriously not going to try and hoodwink me into dropping out of the contest?"

"Hey, if you want to go for it, who am I to stand in your way?"

"Just one of the judges."

And the only person on the show who has your best interests at heart, I thought as her cellphone began to ring.

Chapter Ten

Tiffany

"Hi, what's up, Sinclair?" I asked, recognizing her ringtone.

"You still working?"

"Yes, for about another hour or so."

"Is Ransom there?"

I raised my eyebrows. "Yes, but... how did you know?"

"Look, this reporter friend of Jesse's just gave him a heads-up. The media is headed your way. Channel five, I believe. Apparently, someone called and leaked that Ransom was getting his hair trimmed at *Tangled*."

I groaned. "Oh no."

"Oh no is *right*. They catch you two together, you'll probably get disqualified."

I closed my eyes. "I'm sure."

"You know, it's kind of fishy that he wants you off of the show, suddenly decides to pay you a visit at the shop, and now the media has been tipped off. Sounds like a setup to me."

I turned towards Ransom, who was watching me closely.

Would he actually stoop to that level, and tip off the media just to get me kicked off the show? "Okay, thanks. I'll call you later."

"Damn right you will, girl. Call me back as soon as you can."

I hung up, and shoved my phone into my purse. "Ransom, you have to leave. Now."

Before he could respond, Felicia, who was ringing up Mrs. Conway, stuck her head around the corner. "Girl, we got reporters coming this way.

Ransom's face darkened. "Reporters?"

"Yeah, surprise, surprise," I answered dryly. I walked around the partition and glanced outside of the large plate window. A news van, Channel Five KSLA, was sitting outside of the shop, and standing next to the vehicle was a blonde reporter, powdering her face. "Crap. Can you stall them somehow?"

"Don't worry. I got this," she answered.

"What about them?" I whispered, nodding towards the teens who were both still messing with their phones, and not paying any attention.

She cleared her throat. "Yo, boys. You hungry?"

"Always," replied the dark-haired kid.

"I've got a box of white chocolate-chunk cookies in the break room. You can have them if you want. Just go on back there, and help yourselves."

Smiling, they both stood up and walked towards the back.

"Back there," I said, pointing towards the break room door. "Feel free to turn on the television too. We'll let you know when we're ready for you."

"I guess we're out of here," said Ransom as his security guys joined him.

"Where's your back door?" asked the taller bodyguard.

"The exit is straight back, to the left," I replied.

Ransom grabbed my hand. "Come with us. Like I mentioned before, I'll buy you dinner, and we can catch up."

I snatched my hand back. "No. Now listen to me, Ransom, you may not care about the contest anymore, but I do. Seriously, you've got to get out of here."

"Go away!" hollered Felicia from the front of the store as the reporters tried to enter. "No, I'm *not* unlocking the damn door, fool, we're closed!"

"Please go," I repeated. "Before someone else sees you."

He sighed. "Fine, but –"

"No buts," I answered, walking towards the exit. I opened the door and stuck my head outside. The back parking lot was empty, save for mine and Felicia's cars.

"It's clear," I said, turning around.

Ransom walked towards me.

I moved aside to let him pass, but he stopped, and stared down into my eyes.

"Thanks for the cut," he said with that sexy grin, that always did me in. "And, good luck."

I still wasn't sure if he was responsible for the media showing up. I prayed that he wasn't, and didn't want to believe he was that much of an asshole. "Well, thanks."

He motioned towards his security guards, and they stepped outside, leaving us alone. He then turned back to me. "Taffy," he murmured, stepping closer. "I want you to know that if you need anything, *anything* from me, all you have to do is ask."

I raised my chin, prepared to tell him that all I really wanted was for him to stay away, but before I could answer, he leaned forward, and kissed me.

I forgot about everything else, and kissed him back. Closing my eyes, I melted into the guy I'd fantasized about for the last decade, even before he was a rock star. I forgot about my anger, the media, even the contest as my heart thumped loudly in my chest, and his tongue moved inside of my mouth.

Ohmygod... is this really happening? I thought as I slid my hands around his neck, and into the back of his hair, pulling him closer. His mouth was warm and tasted of mint, which made it even more exhilarating.

Not finding any resistance, his hands slid around my waist, pulling me so close, I could feel his erection.

Knowing that I'd gotten him hard, I felt an intense rush of desire between my legs, and gasped involuntarily.

"Mm..." he groaned, pushing me back gently. "Fuck, I'm so sorry, Taffy. I don't know what got into me."

"It's okay," I replied in a hoarse voice.

He averted his eyes and backed towards the door. "I, uh, I'd better go."

"You should."

Our eyes met again, one more time, and then he left.

"Now what was that?" asked Felicia from behind.

When I turned around, my cheeks were on fire. "How long have you been back there?"

"Long enough to want popcorn," she chuckled. "Damn, girl, I was about ready to turn the hose on you two."

I smiled sheepishly. "I didn't expect it at all. It just kind of happened."

She clucked her tongue. "Celebrities. They think everything is theirs for the taking. You be careful, Tiffany. I don' know what he's up to, but don't let him try and manipulate you."

At that moment, I wanted him to manipulate every single part of me, but wasn't about to give that information up. "I know," I said, walking past her. "So, is the news van gone?"

"No, they're still parked in front."

I crossed my arms under my chest. "I wonder where Ransom and his security guards parked."

"Davenport's Steakhouse, the next block up. I overheard them talking about it."

"Oh."

"Let's get those kids finished up so I can head out of here," said Felicia, looking down at her watch. "I could really use a drink. You sure you don't want to tag along tonight?"

I smiled. "No. Seriously, I'm just going to go home and take it easy. If I make it through the next round of auditions, I'm not going to have a chance to relax for quite a while."

"I hear you. Hey, boys," she said, stepping into the break room. "We're ready for you."

I walked to the front of the shop and looked out of the window just as the news van pulled away from the curb. I wondered if they'd just given up, or if someone had called them off. I thought of Ransom, and how adamant he'd been about me stepping away from the contest. If he had anything to do with the media showing up, I'd never forgive him. I still wasn't sure what his motives were, or why he was so determined to talk me out of continuing on. Regardless, I decided that it would be in my best interest to stay far away from him, at least until the contest was over.

Chapter Eleven

Ransom

After leaving the salon I followed my security guys down the alley and back to the Mercedes.

"Where to now?" asked Bowzer, who was driving.

I rubbed a hand across my face. "I need a drink. Let's hit Bastion's."

Bastion's was a very exclusive bar in West Hollywood, one that I frequented with my band during our downtime. I grabbed my phone and sent a text to Vance to see if he'd meet me there.

"What about Sonia?" asked Jimmy, turning back to look at me. "Aren't you supposed to meet her for dinner tonight?"

I groaned. "That's right. Fuck. I'll just turn off my phone. I'll tell her the battery died, and that I forgot all about dinner. I really can't deal with her shit right now."

"She's going to be pissed," chuckled Bowzer, shaking his head. "I wouldn't want to get on that woman's bad side."

"Oh, hell, I'm used to it," I answered, my mind drifting back to Tiffany, who didn't have a bad side to her. In fact, every side was pretty fucking fantastic.

I laid my head back against the seat and closed my eyes.

What in the hell had I been thinking with that kiss?

The purpose of my visit had been to talk her out of continuing with the contest, not trying to fuck her in the back room. But looking down into her angelic, wholesome face had triggered something inside of me. I wasn't sure if it was the fact that she wasn't trying to seduce me, didn't care that I was famous, or reminded me of the life I'd given up after winning Icon. She definitely represented my past, and the things I'd taken for granted, like a young girl's crush on her friend's older brother, which was much different than the groupies who now threw themselves at me, just because I was a celebrity. This was no longer an adolescent teenager, however. Taffy had grown up into a sexy, young woman and I had to admit, when she returned my kisses, it had turned me on so much, I was still hard.

"So Bastion's then?" asked Bowzer.

I opened my eyes. "Yeah. I need a drink."

***

"Do me a favor and hang back," I told them when we reached Bastion's. "I don't want to draw any attention. If I'm lucky, nobody will recognize me, and I'll have some time to myself."

They both agreed, and while I entered the V.I.P. lounge first, and sat at the bar, they seated themselves at a booth farther away, but still in view.

"What's your poison?" asked the bartender, a hot brunette who'd served me many times in

100

She walked to the television above the bar, and turned it on. The Dodgers were playing at home.

"Thanks."

"No problem. I'll go put that order in for your wings."

"Appreciate it."

I finished my drink and had a couple more while I devoured the wings. After about an hour, I was feeling no pain.

"Hey, Ransom," said Shelly, taking my empty plate away. "Looks like those girls settling in at the bar are checking you out."

I shrugged and looked back at the television. "Good for them."

She raised her eyebrows.

"Sorry," I answered, watching the game. "I'm just not in the mood to socialize. I've got a lot of shit on my mind."

"Too bad, I think one of them is a famous porn star. If not, she should be."

I glanced towards the platinum blonde sitting down at the other end of the bar with another woman whose tits were so big, they needed their own zip code.

Fuck, I thought, recognizing the petite blonde, Amber Drake. I'd made the mistake of banging her more than once, until she'd volunteered to cook me dinner one night. As far as I was concerned, that usually led to spending the entire night together, and brunch with the parents. I hadn't spoken to her since I'd turned down the invitation.

"From the look on your face, you're not interested?"

I swirled the ice around in my drink. "Good observation."

"After a couple more of those, I'll repeat the question, and see if your answer is still the same," she answered before moving towards the women.

I turned my head away from Amber's line of vision, hoping she wouldn't recognize me. She was a nice girl, even for a porn star, but I wasn't interested in plunging my dick into a community pool, when there were much more private ones available. Another image of Tiffany's beautiful smile hit me, and I sighed in frustration.

Why had I kissed her? And even better question, why did I want to do it again?

I had to admit, something about that girl-next-door persona of hers was a definite turn-on. I hadn't had this many hard-ons in one day since the morning I'd found my dad's old girlie magazines, back when I was fifteen.

"The women over there want to buy you another drink," said Shelly, interrupting my thoughts.

I glanced back at Amber and her friend. From the challenging look on her face, she definitely recognized me.

"Shit," I mumbled, turning away.

"Well? What should I tell them?" she asked as I tipped my head back, and tossed back the drink.

I set the glass back onto the bar. "Just tell them that I'm leaving soon. In fact," I said, standing up. "I'd better use the can first." I handed her a hundred dollar bill. "Keep the change."

"Thanks, Ransom."

I stopped by Bowzer's and Jimmy's table on the way to the bathroom. "I'm going to the john, and then we'll leave. Why don't you guys meet me out by the car?"

"No, that's okay," replied Bowzer, his eyes glued at the eye-candy by the bar. "We'll just wait until you're finished, if you don't mind. The view is better inside."

"Your choice," I replied and then walked to the men's room. I stepped inside, grateful to be alone, and relieved myself in the urinal. As I was zipping up my fly, I heard someone else enter the bathroom. I turned to wash my hands, swore under my breath.

"Hey, stranger," said Amber, leaning against the doorway, wearing a miniscule black dress that barely covered the top of her thighs, and silver platform shoes that showed off her spray-tanned legs.

I cleared my throat. "Amber. What's going on?"

With a wicked smile, she began moving towards me. "I just thought I'd catch you before you left."

I turned on the faucet and began washing my hands. "Couldn't you wait until I left the bathroom to say 'hi'?"

She stopped next to me, and our eyes met in the mirror. "Okay, you got me. I guess I just wanted some privacy."

Remembering how she enjoyed fucking in public places, I quickly stepped around her, and turned on the hand dryer. I wasn't about to go down that path. Not with her. "Oh?"

She pulled her hair over her shoulder. "Guess I've missed you, you know?"

I shrugged. "You have my number."

"Funny, I must have your *old* number because the last time I called, a stranger answered, and said he'd never heard of you."

"Yeah, my number changes frequently. Stalkers and all," I replied, holding back a smirk. The last time she'd called, I'd had a buddy answer the phone for me. It was the only thing that had stopped her continuous texts and phone calls.

Her eyes trailed over me appraisingly and she licked her glossy lips. "Damn, Ransom, you look as sexy as ever. I love the new haircut, by the way. Can I touch your head?"

"I'd prefer not," I answered, although I began questioning my self-control when her eyes lowered to my zipper.

"Oh, you're no fun," she pouted, leaning forward. She touched my chest with her brightly colored manicured nail. "I remember when you used to be loads of fun. Or should I say..." her finger trailed all the way down to my crotch. "When guy in here used to be in charge of the fun."

I grabbed her hand firmly. "Stop, Amber."

She licked her upper lip seductively. "You want me," she whispered, now touching the front of my jeans with her other hand. She ran her finger over the hard outline of my dick. "This guy never lies."

I grabbed both of her hands. "Amber, it's over."

Her face fell. "What is your problem? From what I hear, you've got a whore in your room practically every night, and what – I'm not good enough, now?"

"It has nothing to do with that," I said, stepping away from her. "Look, I've got to go."

She grabbed my forearm. "Wait! Ransom, you know, I really thought we had something special. I thought you did, too."

I sighed. "We had fun, but it's over. You've got to let it go."

She dug her nails into my skin. "You think because you're this hotshot celebrity now, that you can just treat women like trash? Throw them away whenever you're finished with them?"

I pulled my arm away. "Jesus, Amber, you're overreacting. We had sex a few times, okay? We never even dated."

Her lips trembled. "Yeah, I know. I wasn't even good enough to buy dinner for."

"I'm not going to argue with you. I've got to go," I said, backing away. "Look, I'm sorry you thought there was more to what we had, but honestly, I never promised you anything. Hell, you were the one who jumped my bones without even asking the rules."

"The rules?!" she snapped. "So, it was just a *game* for you?"

I groaned. "No, it wasn't. I didn't mean it that way."

"You know what? You're a real fucking prick, Ransom," she answered, kicking one of the stalls angrily. "You don't fucking deserve me anyway."

"You're probably right," I said, opening the door. Without another glance, I left the bathroom, relieved that I'd ended it with her when I did. If she was this obsessed after a few tumbles in the sack, I could only imagine what would have happened if I'd have actually accepted a home-cooked meal from her. Hell, it wasn't as if she'd been some naïve, young woman who'd been taken advantage of. There was nothing pure or wholesome about Amber. From what I'd remembered, she'd pursued me hard, and fucked me even harder, which I thought had worked well for the both of us. I was obviously wrong.

"Hey, Ransom! What's up, brother?" hollered Vance in his gravelly voice. He was sitting at the bar with his twin, Kurt, who I noticed was now ogling Amber's friend's tits, along with everyone else at the bar. Both guys were dressed in the usual biker attire of ripped jeans, leather vests, and bandanas covering their long, red hair.

I walked back over to the bar, and shook both of their hands. "I didn't think you guys were going to show. I sent you a message about two hours ago."

"Fuck, I tried calling you back but your phone must be dead or something," replied Vance, scratching his red goatee. He stared at my head, and smirked. "Aw... man, why in the hell did you go and do that for?"

I ran a hand through the top. "Like it?"

Kurt snorted. "You look like a fucking executive at IBM or Lockheed Martin. What, you in the market for sophisticated putang now that you're back on Icon again?"

"Hell, Ransom, could get any putang he wanted, haircut or not," said Vance, lowering his voice. "Wouldn't surprise me if he's already had every piece of ass in this place."

"Since there are only about five broads here," replied Kurt. "You're probably right. But I tell you what," he lowered his voice and looked over at Amber's friend lecherously. "If Ransom can get me in good with that chick there, hell, I'll shave my head, too. Fuck, I'll shave both of them."

"Isn't that the girl you were dating a few months back?" asked Vance, as Amber sat back down, her eyes stabbing me viciously from across the bar.

"Yeah," I answered, turning away.

"She looks pissed. Shelly just poured her a shot of tequila, too." He chuckled. "You know what that means?"

My cue to leave. A pissed off woman and tequila were not a good mix.

"I'll catch you guys later," I said, nodding towards my security guys, who immediately stood up.

"We just got here," replied Vance, surprised. "Come on. Have one drink with us."

I glanced back over towards Amber who was staring at me as Shelly poured her another shot. "Sorry, next time. I've got something important I need to do."

"You mean with Sonia?" asked Vance. "She called me looking for you."

"No, and if she calls again, do me a favor and don't tell her you saw me."

"You can tell her yourself when you get home. She was pissed off and headed towards your place last time I talked to her. About an hour ago."

I sighed. "Great."

"Ransom, what's up with all of the pissed off women?" smirked Kurt. "You need help putting a smile on their faces, I'd be happy to volunteer."

"If it were only that easy," I replied.

Vance chuckled. "Ransom's always on some woman's shit-list. Hell," he pulled out his wallet. "I wouldn't doubt if there was a bounty on your head with all of the girls you've kicked out of your bed."

I scowled. "Fuck that. I'm not *that* bad."

"Are you kidding me? What about last summer when three chicks were fighting over you on the bus? Two of them ended up in the E.R.

One had a broken nose and the other had a concussion," replied Vance.

"They were all crazy," I replied, remembering that nightmare. I'd passed out with two chicks in my bed, while another girl I'd had the previous night somehow made it back onto the tour bus. She'd launched herself at the naked girls, and I'd barely made it out of bed unscathed myself.

"So, what happened with the third one? She get *the* prize?" asked Kurt, grinning wickedly.

"What she got was kicked off of the bus," I said.

Vance burst out laughing. "Yeah, but that was after she got down on her knees..."

"Bullshit," I interrupted, although my mind had been pretty muddled that night.

"You were so fucked up you don't even remember," replied Vance. "I walked in on her blowing you, man. Not more than fifteen minutes later."

"Fuck, she owed me for those expensive sheets she ruined by giving one of the girls a bloody nose," I protested as the memory came back. She'd gotten down on her knees and begged to make it up to me. It was only fair."

Vance took a sip of his drink. "Anyway, the point is, Kurtis, when you're a celebrity women are *always* throwing themselves at you. Obviously you're going to piss some of them off when they find out it's just sex, and nothing more."

"How come you don't have women problems like that?" asked Kurt, staring at his brother. "Hell, you're the drummer."

"Have you looked at your mug in the mirror lately?" he chuckled. "We ain't pretty. Not like Rans, here."

"That, and Billie Jean," I replied.

Billie Jean was his fiancée. She was also spunky, intelligent, and beautiful. Ever since Vance had met her, he'd turned down many free pieces of ass.

"Damn right," said Vance. "I've had enough tail in my life to know that once you find someone with more than just a nice pair of tits and a great ass, you hold on to her. No way am I going to fuck up something special like that just to wax my dick when we're on the road."

"Maybe that's what you need, Ransom," said Kurt. "A woman to keep you out of trouble."

"Right. Women *are* the trouble," I replied.

"I'll take that kind of trouble, any day," said Kurt looking back over at Amber's friend.

"You can have it," I said as Amber stood up, swaying slightly. She said something to her friend, who looked at me and snorted.

"I'll catch you later," I said as she began staggering towards us.

"Better call security," laughed Vance. "Before she gets her hands on you, and fucks up that pretty face."

"Yeah, you run away again!" she called as Bowzer and Jimmy walked me outside. "You fucking asshole!"

Chapter Twelve

Tiffany

It was after seven-thirty by the time I made it back to my one-bedroom apartment in Stanton, only twenty minutes away from the shop. At the last minute, I'd stopped at a video store, and picked up a movie, *Safe Haven,* which I'd been meaning to see for several months.

I set the movie on the coffee table, and grabbed the growing stack of bills from my counter. With a sigh, I fell into my mauve chaise, thankful I'd splurged for it the previous month. Everything else I owned was second-hand, including the eighties-style ugly, brown leather sofa sitting across from me. My next few checks would definitely go towards more new furnishings. If I was going to spend a lot of time alone in my apartment, at least I could enjoy the view.

As I finished opening the mail, my stomach began to growl, reminding me that I'd forgotten to eat lunch. Felicia's cookies had all but disappeared by the time the teens had left the salon, and now I was so hungry, I could barely see straight. I stood up, and went into the kitchen to heat up a frozen meal from the freezer. As I reached inside for a package of pasta, my cell phone went off. I set the box on the counter, and grabbed the phone from my purse. The number displayed wasn't one I recognized.

"Hello?"

"Taffy?"

Oh hell.

Ransom.

"Yes." I pulled my hair to the side and walked back over to the counter. "So, I thought we agreed to stop communicating?"

"I don't specifically remember agreeing to that."

"Ransom..."

"Look, I just forgot to pay you," he said quickly. "That's really why I'm calling."

I picked up the fettuccini. "Don't worry about it," I said, opening up the cardboard box.

"Hey, I don't feel right about this. What's your address? I'll swing by and drop the money off."

"No," I protested. "Obviously, that's not a good idea."

"Still worried, huh? Look, nobody has recognized me now that my hair is different. In fact, I've been hanging around at Bastion's and even the bartender didn't recognize me."

"You're at a bar?"

"Yeah."

"Hmm..," I said, turning on the microwave. "You know, if you really feel that strongly about paying me, just mail a check directly to the shop."

"They can be tracked. Obviously, my name would be on the check."

"True. Just forget it then. It's not a big deal."

"Bullshit. You need to get paid. Let me bring it over. I promise to be a complete gentleman."

I thought about that kiss in the shop, and it made my belly tingle. In fact, the thought of being alone with him in my apartment was already giving me some wicked ideas. I should have shut him down right there. Told him to go home and to not worry about it.

But not me.

Not the girl who would have once done anything to be alone with Ransom. Obviously, I was still *that* girl. "Okay."

He paused. "Okay?"

"Yes, okay," I replied, reminding myself that I needed the money anyway, especially during the competition when I wouldn't be working. Hell, maybe I *was* being a little paranoid about him coming over. It wasn't as if someone had my apartment bugged or monitored.

I gave him my address.

"Great, I'll be there within the next hour. Are you hungry? I could pick up a pizza along the way."

I stared at the microwave. I had to admit, pizza sounded a lot better than a rubbery frozen meal. "Sure, that sounds good."

"Awesome. What do you like on your pizza?"

"Everything but –"

"Anchovies," he finished.

"Yeah, how did you know?"

"Oh, come on... all of those sleepovers you and Remy had together?"

I laughed. "That's right, and you used to eat all of the leftover pizza for breakfast, before we woke up. I remember how furious it made Remy."

I also remembered how hot he looked in his flannel pajama bottoms. I pictured his broad shoulders, sculpted pecs, and sexy abs bending over the pizza box all of those Saturday mornings, and my mouth watered.

"I used to love it cold, and haven't had any for years. We order pizzas all the time when we're touring, but there usually aren't any leftovers. The guys are like garbage disposals."

"Your band members?"

"Yeah and the roadies. Those guys can eat."

"What about the groupies?"

He chuckled. "They aren't usually there for the pizza."

"I imagine not."

I wondered how friendly he was with the groupies, and felt a stab of jealously, which I *knew* was ridiculous because, *hello*, he was a celebrity. Heck, he probably had sex with a different girl every night.

And I was tripping?

Pathetic...

"You still there?"

I cleared my throat. "Okay, yeah, so I'll see you in a little while? Just to warn you, though, you can't stay long. I rented a chick-flick, and have to get up early tomorrow morning."

"Hey, I'm down with chick-flicks."

"Since when?" I snorted. "You used to tease the hell out of us when we'd rent them."

"I just liked teasing you."

I paused. "That hasn't changed."

"Nope."

I smiled. "It's getting late. So, I'll see you soon I guess?"

"No backing out now."

"Right."

After hanging up, I threw away the frozen meal, made a dash for the bathroom, and took a quick shower. When I was finished, I slipped on a pair of white shorts and a light blue laced Jersey tank-top, pulled my hair up into a ponytail, and then applied some pink lip-gloss. When I was satisfied, I raced back into the living room, straightened up as much as possible, and lit two vanilla scented candles. As I was putting the lighter away, the envelope from American Icon caught my eye. I'd read through the most of the packet last night but not the small print, which I knew would include the rules of the contest, and probably a stringent clause about not socializing with the judges.

Sighing, I pulled out the packet, and began reviewing the pages I'd missed.

"Damn."

Sure enough, it stated very clearly that any interaction away from the show with the judges, camera crew, or anyone else associated with American Icon was prohibited, and the penalty was exactly what I'd imagined – disqualification.

I sat back and sighed.

Disqualification.

In black and white.

Well, no questioning it now.

Grabbing my cell phone, I called Ransom back.

"You can't come over here, Ransom."

"Too late," he replied. "I'm just entering your lobby. In fact, can you buzz me up?"

I closed my eyes, and groaned. "No, Ransom. Call your guys back, please. If someone sees you here, I just know that I'm going to get disqualified. Hell, I've probably screwed myself by cutting your hair in the shop earlier."

"Taffy, calm down."

I began to pace. "I can't."

He lowered his voice. "Do you have a roommate or nosy neighbors?"

"No."

"Then who do you think is going to notice me?"

I stopped. "I... oh, my God! What if you were followed?"

He chuckled. "I'm not a criminal being investigated."

"But you're famous. Don't you have the paparazzi following you everywhere?" I asked, looking out the window, and down below towards the street.

"They've never followed me."

"You're lying. I've seen you on television getting angry with them."

"I don't recall that."

"Maybe you were trashed?" An image of him flipping them the bird came to mind. And another, where he was seen pushing a cameraman out of his face and telling him to 'fuck off'.

"Maybe. My guys have already dropped me off, and I'm holding a hot pizza, and a bottle of red wine. Better let me up before someone *does* notice me hanging out here by your mailbox."

I placed a hand on my forehead. "Fine. I'm apartment three-twenty-four. Go straight up the stairs, and it's the first apartment on the left."

"Top floor?"

"Yes," I said, pushing the buzzer.

Less than a minute later, I was pulling him into my apartment. "This is such a mistake." I said, slamming and locking the door.

His lips curled up. "I don't think I've ever heard a woman say that to me before."

"This is totally different, and you know it." I bit my lip and looked through the peephole. "Are you sure nobody followed you?"

"Yes, I'm positive. Relax."

I turned around. "Easy for you to say."

"Where do you want this?" he asked, holding up the wine and pizza.

"I'll take that," I replied, grabbing the bottle. "Just put the pizza box on the coffee table. I'll go and grab some plates."

"Okay. I hope you like Dolcetto."

My eyes widened. "Dol, what?"

"The wine. It's a Dolcetto. I heard it goes great with pizza. I'm a beer and tequila drinker myself."

"Oh. Well, thanks for getting it. Would you like me to pour you a glass, too?"

He sat down on the sofa. "Sure, I'll try some."

"Okay. I'll be right back," I said, walking into the kitchen with the wine. Once inside, I uncorked the wine, and filled two glasses.

"You need any help?"

I sucked in my breath, and turned to find him standing close.

Too close.

I backed up to the counter. "I didn't even hear you walk in."

With an amused grin, he moved closer, and grabbed the glasses. As he did, he bent close to my neck, his lips only inches away. "You smell great," he whispered, his warm breath on my skin.

"Uh, thanks," I replied, feeling a tingle run down my body.

He straightened up, and turned around. "Don't forget the plates," he said, leaving the kitchen.

Trying to compose myself, I opened up the cupboard and grabbed a couple of my mother's china plates, the ones with the blue flowers that she'd cherished so much. No matter how nervous I was, this night was special. Not only did I have a celebrity in my apartment, but it was *him.*

Ransom.

I may never get this chance again.

I followed him back into the living room, and paused for a second, watching as he sat down.

Damn if he didn't make my ugly sofa look good.

"So, um, if you aren't feeling like a movie," I said, sitting down next to him, "we could just have dinner?"

He opened up the box of pizza, and grabbed one of the plates. "You're still trying to get rid of me, aren't you?"

I smirked. "You got me."

He flashed me a dimpled smile. "Relax, babe," he replied, handing me a plate filled with pizza. "I'm already here, in your apartment, and nobody else knows about it."

"Your bodyguards know."

"Actually, to tell you the truth, they don't know I'm visiting someone affiliated with the show. Fact is, I told them I was chilling at buddy's place."

"Well, when are they picking you up?"

"Whenever I tell them to." He smiled wickedly. "So, Taffy, I guess that means I'm *yours* for the entire night."

He may have been teasing me, but I didn't miss the message in his eyes. He was offering more than just pizza, and watching carefully for my reaction.

Chapter Thirteen

Ransom

The blush on her cheeks was priceless, making me want her even more. I couldn't have been stiffer if I were a corpse.

Down, boy.

"Would you just stop," she laughed nervously.

"Now what fun would that be?" I asked, my eyes traveling to her tank top, which hugged her round breasts in a way that was making my mouth water. I found myself wondering if the rosy color of Tiffany's cheeks matched her nipples, and was immediately sprung.

"Excuse me, my eyes are up here," she said, looking at me in disbelief. "I just can't believe you."

I reached over, and brushed a strand of blond hair from her lip. "Sorry, I was distracted for a second. Anyway, admit it. You like it when I check you out."

Her jaw dropped. "You are *so* arrogant."

"I have to hold on to something," I replied with a smirk.

"Right."

I looked around her apartment, which was small but homey, and sighed. "This is nice, isn't it? Eating pizza, watching a rented movie, doing... normal things."

She shrugged. "Yeah, I suppose."

"Well, you might not appreciate it as much as I do because *normal* isn't a part of my life, anymore. So when random *normalness* happens, it's... kind of, I don't know... cool."

"Oh."

I grabbed a piece of pizza, and raised it to my lips. "Dig in," I said, before biting down. "You're safe, I left out the anchovies."

"Okay, but I'm warning you, excessive carbs make me a little crazy."

I smiled. "What about *wine* and excessive carbs?"

Her eyes lit up. "I've been known to dance on tables, sing too loud, and –"

"Get naked?" I interrupted, wiggling my eyebrows.

She clucked her tongue and sighed. "Oh boy."

"Sorry. After what happened earlier today, I can't seem to get my mind out of the gutter."

"Yeah, about that," she said, looking embarrassed. "I'm sorry."

"It wasn't *your* fault," I said. "In fact, I pretty much attacked you."

She lifted her glass from the coffee table. "Well, I wasn't exactly fighting you off."

"I didn't think you would."

"Oh, is that so?"

"Come on, Taffy, just admit it, you've always had a thing for me," I joked.

Her left eyebrow arched. "Excuse me?"

"It's true," I said, enjoying the fire in her eyes. I'd almost forgotten how much fun it was to get her riled. "Hell, you're undressing me with your eyes right now."

Her jaw dropped. "Oh, my God! You are *so* obnoxious *and* conceited."

"And sexy," I said with a cocky grin. "You left that part out."

Her cheeks flushed. "Okay, fine! I'll admit that I may have had a crush on you when I was young and very naive, but that was then, and this is now."

I put my plate on the coffee table. "Really?" I asked, turning towards her. I put my arm on the back of the sofa, and leaned closer, "because that kiss earlier, it was pretty fucking intense. I find it hard to believe that it didn't mean anything at all."

"It didn't." She sat up straighter. "You caught me off guard, and well, it's been a while since anyone's kissed me."

"A girl as beautiful as you, I find it hard to believe."

"I haven't been exactly looking for a boyfriend, and I don't hook up with guys just for... just for sex. Not like what you're used to, I'm sure."

"I respect that," I said, which was the truth. "More than you know."

She stared at me for a minute and sighed. "I've grown up, Ransom, and I'm certainly not one of those star-struck groupies who'll bend to your every whim. What happened earlier was a mistake. In every way."

I scratched my head. "Wow, you sure know how to crush a guy's ego."

Her eyes twinkled. "Somehow I'm sure *you'll* get over it."

"You must think I'm a real shit," I said. "That I jump into bed with any willing chick, and then forget about her the next day?"

"Don't you?"

I grinned. "Actually, it's the other way around, they jump into *my* bed. But, I'll admit, I do forget about them the next day. Most of the girls that end up in my bed *are* very forgettable."

"Wow... you're nice."

"Oh, hell, they're only after me because of what I represent, Taffy. I'm famous, and I have a shitload of money. Do any of them ever ask what my favorite color is, if I like to read, or hell, why I have a scar on my chest? No, they only care about what's below the belt, one of which is my wallet and the other, I don't think I have to spell it out for you."

"How is that, by the way?"

I arched my eyebrow and grinned wickedly. "If you really want to know..."

She rolled her eyes. "No, you goofball, your heart."

I'd been born with a hole in my heart, one that they'd repaired with surgery, when I was very young. There hadn't been any complications, and from what I'd been told growing up, it was nothing to worry about.

"Well, it hasn't been broken yet."

"Not what I meant."

"I'm fine. Never been any problems."

"Should you be drinking?"

I picked up the glass of wine, and took a drink. "Isn't wine supposed to be good for your health?"

"I have no idea, but if it really is, then I'm assuming it should be done in moderation."

"Are you also assuming that I don't do it in moderation?"

"Something tells me that there's nothing you do in moderation."

I put a hand over my chest. "Now *that* hurts. You're a cruel, cruel woman."

"Eat your pizza, it's getting cold."

I smiled.

My cell phone started ringing, and I cursed myself for not turning it back off the moment I walked into her apartment. I took it out of my jeans and sighed.

Remy.

"It's my sister. Something must be up. She never calls me at night"

"Then you'd better answer it. It might be really important."

I wasn't sure why, but I felt like a cloud of doom had settle over us. I answered anyway. "Hey, Remy, what's going on?"

She was sobbing. "Ransom..."

I tensed up. "What's wrong?"

"It's mom," she moaned. "She's been killed!"

Chapter Fourteen

Tiffany

Ransom's face went completely white. "What?" he mumbled hoarsely into the phone. After a few seconds, he stood up, and turned his back to me. There was no mistaking the way his shoulders slumped, that something was very wrong. After a few muffled words, his shoulders began to shake, and I could tell he was crying.

I got off the sofa and touched his arm, trying to give him some kind of comfort. I had no idea what Remy was saying, but it was wrecking him.

"Okay," he said, turning away from me again. "I'll see you in a few hours. Love you, too."

"What's wrong?" I asked after he hung up, and faced me with glassy eyes.

"I have to leave," he said, his voice thick.

"What happened? What's wrong?"

His face crumbled. "My mother was murdered. I have to go."

I stared at him in horror. "What?!"

He started punching numbers into his phone. "They don't know what happened. The housekeeper found her. Someone... shot her."

I covered my mouth. "I'm so sorry, Ransom."

"I have to leave," he mumbled, putting the phone to his ear. "Yeah, it's me. I need you guys to pick me back up. Yes, right now. Something's come up." He hung up and turned back to me.

"I'm going to wait downstairs for the car," he said. "Sorry about cutting this short."

I put my hand on his arm. "Ransom, I'm *so* sorry. I loved Carol. God, she was such a wonderful woman. I wish there was something I could do for you and Remy."

His eyes flashed angrily. "Me, too. I wish I could find the bastard who did this, shoot him in the face, and then run him over with my car before shooting him in the face again."

"Hopefully the cops will find out who did this, and bring some kind of justice."

"They'd better," he said in a clipped voice. He backed up and avoided my eyes again. "I'll call you, and let you know what I find out."

I took a deep breath, closed the distance between us, and threw my arms around him. "I'm here for you and Remy. Call me no matter what, okay?"

His body relaxed, and he slid his arms around me. "Thanks, Taffy," he whispered into my hair.

I closed my eyes. If there was one thing I knew, Ransom loved Carol more than life itself, and the pain had to be devastating. "Anytime, Ransom."

He squeezed me tightly, and then let me go. "I'll call you."

I nodded and watched him leave.

***

Carol's murder was all over the news the following day, along with photos of Ransom and Remy as they tried to avoid the media going to and from their parents' home. Rumors of the murder had also spread like wildfire, most of it being that it was a hate crime against Ransom. As a celebrity, I knew he had to have a lot of enemies, some of them seriously psychotic, and it made me wonder if continuing with Icon was a mistake. Right now my life was simple, and the only people I pissed off were clients who didn't like the way their hair had turned out, and thankfully, that was a rare occurrence.

I called Remy in the morning and left my condolences on her voicemail. When she returned my call later in the day, I could tell that she was barely holding it together.

"Tiffany, the funeral is in four days. You're coming, right?"

"Of course, Rem."

She paused. "I figured, but just wanted to know for sure."

"How are you holding up?"

"I'll be better when Taylor arrives. He's in Florida right now, doing some kind of promotional thing for Icon."

"When's he getting back?"

"Tonight," she answered, sniffling. "Hold on," she said and then blew her nose. "Sorry."

"Don't worry about it, silly. Listen, if you need *anything*, let me know."

"I just need to see you soon, Tiff. We're having a private wake the night before the funeral. Can you make that, too?"

"I'll do my best."

She gave me the address, and I wrote it down. I knew I had appointments, but there was no way I'd disappoint her, and decided to call my clients as quickly as possible, to reschedule.

"How's Ransom doing?"

She snorted. "He left early this morning, and then came back, drunk. He passed out about four hours ago in his old room, and is still sleeping."

"I'm sure this is hard for everyone."

"Right," she mumbled. "He's hardly visited her at all these past few months, and he lives in California, for God's sake."

"Doesn't he travel a lot?"

"Yes, but he still could have seen her a number of times. Obviously, he was too busy partying and raising hell. It just makes me so sick sometimes, you know? Just because he's famous now doesn't give him an excuse to be a jackass."

"I don't think he's very happy."

"Boo hoo," she muttered. "He now has everything he's always wanted, and if that doesn't make him happy, then he seriously needs help."

Not wanting to upset her further, I changed the subject. "Okay forget Ransom, how are you *really* doing?"

She released a shaky breath. "I miss her so much. I mean we talked on the phone every day, and she was always there for me. *Always*. God, I keep checking my phone, expecting to see a missed call from her or a text." Her voice hitched. "I just don't know how I'm going to get through my wedding or anything else without her at my side."

"You will, sweetie. And *she* would want you to keep living," I said, remembering how I'd said these same words to myself when my own mother had died. It had become my daily mantra, and although I'd had a hard time believing in it at first, over time it had helped me cope.

"I know you've been through this," she said softly. "And I wish I would have been there for you, knowing how much pain you went through. I feel like such a selfish bitch."

"No… no… no. You had your own grief to deal with," I replied. "I didn't expect anything from you and… it was something that I had to deal with myself. Just like with your mom. It's great having friends and family with you, but at night, when you're lying in bed and thinking about the person you lost, that's when you realize that *you* have to be strong. Just remember that I'm always here for you. No matter the distance, no matter the hour. You call me if you need to talk."

"I love you, Tiff," she said softly. "And I've missed you."

"I love you, too, Rem. Don't worry, you'll get through this. It hurts, and the pain feels like it's never going to end, but you'll get through this. Just take it one day at a time."

"I hope so. One moment I feel numb, like I can't cry another tear, the next, I feel like my heart has been ripped out of my chest. It's horrible."

"I know."

It had been hell for me, too, especially when I had to go through all of her things. The photographs, the familiar scent of perfume in her sweaters, and all of the silly things I'd made for her in school that she'd cherished and kept. It was then that the finality of it really hit me hard. My mom was gone, and never coming back.

She blew her nose again. "Oh... Taylor is trying to call, I'd better answer it. I'll call you later."

"Only if you have a chance. I know you're busy with everything."

"Never too busy for you. I'm not making any more mistakes with our friendship, Tiff."

I smiled. Sometimes it took a loss to appreciate what you still had. "You didn't make any mistakes, hon. Just remember that."

"Regardless, I'll call you later."

"Okay."

After we hung up, I scarfed down a turkey sandwich, and then greeted my last customer of the day. After determining what she wanted, I went into the backroom to search for a suitable hair color, when Sinclair stormed in.

"Dammit, I'm done with men," she snarled, clenching her teeth. She was pacing, and had her cell phone gripped tightly in her hand.

"What's wrong?"

Stopping, she folded her arms under her chest and leaned back against the wall. "Reed. I haven't been able to get ahold of him, and Jesse said he's not returning any of his calls either."

"Is he in court, or with a client?" I asked. It was four o'clock and that didn't seem unreasonable.

"No. Well, not that I know of. It's just…"

"What?"

She sighed. "We got into this argument last night after he was late for dinner. We argued, and then he left. Well, I more or less *kicked* him out."

"Oh, my God, why?"

She stared down at her sandals. "I was pissed. I'd planned this romantic evening for the both of us, and had warned him about being late, that I had something very important that I wanted to tell him. Well," she looked up, "he didn't show up until after nine, and his excuse was that he had to give that bimbo assistant of his a ride home because her car was in the shop."

"Ah," I replied.

"What pisses me off is that he was supposed to be home by seven-thirty." Her lips thinned. "I guess that after he drove chesty home, she asked if he could look at her computer, because it *supposedly* had a virus or something. Claimed she couldn't get into her work files. So, obviously, he had to stick around and help the little witch."

"Did he call you?"

"No. He said he lost track of time."

I raised my eyebrows.

"I think the only virus that woman has is between her legs," she mumbled, tears in her eyes. "I've seen the way she stares at him. Like he's the last man on Earth, and it's her mission to repopulate the planet. And obviously, he's clueless. Dammit, why are men so clueless? *Especially* Reed?"

I wanted to point out that it was possible they weren't as clueless as she presumed, but that would probably piss her off even more.

"Do you trust him?"

"I want to. I really do. But Jesse says that I should just forget about Reed, now too," she wiped a tear from her cheek. "He doesn't think Reed will change. Thinks he's always going to be a player. How am I supposed to trust someone whose own brother thinks he's a scoundrel?"

"Good point, but he doesn't sleep with Reed, and he doesn't know what's really in his brother's heart. What do you feel in *your* heart?"

She smiled bitterly. "I don't know. It's my head that's telling me to be careful. I've learned that my heart is gullible, and to not always trust it."

"Have you accused him of cheating to his face?"

"It kind of came out last night. I didn't exactly accuse him of cheating, though. I did accuse him of being easily manipulated by women."

"So he left?"

"Well," she smiled sheepishly. "I kind of pressured him to leave after he stuck up for Nina, and said that I was being ridiculous."

"I don't know what to tell you," I said, resting my hand on her shoulder. "My experience with guys hasn't been all that good either."

"Men are fucking pricks," replied Thane, the owner of Tangled, as he walked into the backroom, filling the small space with his massive frame. "That's all you need to know."

"You've mentioned that before, Mufasa," chuckled Sinclair. "But your own actions prove otherwise."

With his shoulder-length blonde hair and golden eyes, we referred to him as "The Lion King", not only because of his ruggedly handsome looks, but the fact that he was very protective of all of us. Especially after Sera, our nail technician, had ended up in the hospital after being attacked in her garage a couple of weeks earlier. Not only had he paid for a new security system for her home, but he spent a lot of evenings there as well, making us wonder if there was something more going on between them.

He grabbed a broom and dustpan. "That's because I don't mix business and pleasure. It's a very bad combination."

"What about Sera?" I teased.

"Sera? She doesn't mix business and pleasure either. At least, as far as I know."

"Right," chuckled Sinclair.

He cocked an eyebrow. "What's that supposed to mean?"

"Oh, nothing," she said innocently.

"Look, there's nothing going on with Sera and me. She's had enough problems with men, and doesn't need another guy intruding on her life."

"Oh, that's too bad, because I think you and Sera would make such a cute couple," replied Sinclair.

His eyes softened. "Cute? Oh, hell. She's too good for a schmuck like me."

"Don't be so hard on yourself," said Sinclair. "From what we see, you're all talk and really just a big teddy bear."

He reached over, and tugged one of her red curls. "Looks can be deceiving. Hell, if you girls knew about my past, you'd probably look for a new job."

"Oh, come on," said Sinclair. "I'm sure that whatever you did can't be all that bad."

"You have no idea."

"Why don't you tell us and we can decide," I prodded, wondering what he was hiding.

He grinned. "Sorry. It's classified information. If I tell you..."

"You'd have to shoot us?" I finished.

He smiled and ignored the question. "Anyway, I'm not proud of what I've done, but doing something for Sera, like being a temporary watchdog, makes me somehow feel like I'm redeeming myself."

"Do they know who attacked her yet?" I asked.

His lips tightened. "She thinks it's her ex-husband, but can't prove it, and the police can't seem to find the son-of-a-bitch."

I thought of Sera's young daughter, and grimaced. "Wow. Poor Sera and Emma."

He nodded. "Emma is an amazing little girl, though. She deserves so much more than that bastard for a father. I hope she never has to see him again."

"That's so sad," I said.

"But true. He's dangerous," said Thane.

Sinclair sighed. "So, men are pricks. Are you talking from personal experience?"

He smirked. "I'm not going to lie. I've been a piece of shit to women in the past. I've cheated, lied, and have used women for whatever means I needed at the time."

"Wow," replied Sinclair. "I wouldn't go sharing this information. Especially if you want any sympathy from us or help finding dates."

"I'm not asking for anything, I'm just warning you both to be careful. Most guys are out for one thing – themselves. Anyway, you'd better get out to your customer, Tiffany," he said, looking out the door. "She looks a little irritated."

I grabbed the swatches I'd selected and raced past him. "Crap, I forgot."

I'd also forgotten to ask Sinclair what the important news was that she had for Reed.

Chapter Fifteen

Tiffany

I got off early on Thursday, and drove to Borgenstein's Funeral Home, which was only about twenty minutes from the shop. Turning off the radio, I looked down at my clothing, and wondered if my black, lacy camisole was too revealing under the dark linen suit I'd picked out. I hadn't thought much about it, until I'd caught one of my older male customers leering at my cleavage when I'd trimmed his bangs earlier. I'd never sped through a haircut so fast in my life. Knowing that it was too late to do anything about the outfit, I shrugged it off and pulled my car into the parking lot.

"Great," I muttered, noticing the reporters surrounding the entrance. Fortunately, the family had also hired security, and the guests were being ushered quickly inside of the building.

"Can I see your I.D.?" asked the tall lot attendant, who was holding a clipboard. He reminded me of an actor my mother used to go crazy for, Sam Elliot, back when his hair was still dark, and he was kicking guys out of bars on television.

I handed him my driver's license and he checked my name against the list.

"You're good to go, darlin'," he said, his lips curling up.

I stared at him in awe; he even *sounded* like Sam Elliot. "That's a relief. Um, has anyone ever told you that you look and sound just like Sam Elliot?"

He chuckled. "Let's just say it hasn't hurt my love life any. My first name is Sam, by the way."

My eyebrows shot up. "You're kidding?"

"Short for Sampson," he said, holding out his hand.

I laughed and shook it. "Nice to meet you. You already know my name."

"Yep, and I won't be forgettin' it any time soon," he replied with a twinkle in his blue eyes. "Now, little lady, park over to your left and I'll have someone usher you inside."

"Thanks, Sam."

"Anytime, Tiffany. Anytime," he replied, stepping back from my car.

I parked the car, and then was escorted by two other security men.

"Excuse me, Miss?" prodded one of the reporters as I was ushered towards the doorway. "How do you know the deceased? Are you a family member?"

I kept my face down and stepped into the main foyer of the building, where the familiar smell of despair and carnations made my heart ache for my friends.

"Tiffany?"

I turned to the sound of Ransom's voice, and found him walking up a flight of stairs. My heart skipped a beat as he moved towards me with his hands in his pockets.

"Well, you certainly clean up nice," I
blurted out loud, like an idiot.

He looked down, and I felt really foolish as
I thought of *why* he'd dressed up. There was no
denying it, however; he looked very striking in his
black tailored suit. Like some kind of G.Q. model.
He smiled grimly. "Thanks."

"Uh, sure," I answered, still feeling a little
foolish.

He tilted his head. "Remy said you'd be
here, but I didn't know for sure. With the contest
and all..."

"This is more important than the contest,"
I answered quickly. "Your mother means more to
me than any contest."

He nodded. "I appreciate you coming."

I licked my lips "I'm so sorry for you loss."

"Thanks. Me too," he answered with a
hitched voice.

I stared up into his eyes, and the despair
reflected there broke my heart. He looked like a
lost little boy, and I desperately wanted to wrap
my arms around him, tell him that it would be
okay, that I'd be there for him as long as he
needed me. "Ransom, I –"

"Tiffany?"

I turned around, and was immediately
engulfed by Remy, who was three inches taller
than me without heels. "Oh, Rem," I said, as she
hugged me tightly.

"I'm so glad you're here," she said,
releasing me. "Mom would be happy too, that you
came."

"I wouldn't have missed it," I said, looking up at her.

"You look the same," she smiled sadly, as she wiped her nose with a tissue. "Actually, I lied. You look more beautiful than ever."

"No, *you* look beautiful," I countered. And it was true. With her dark ebony hair, gray eyes, and high cheekbones, she looked a lot like her brother.

"Thanks. I'd better bring you in to see her. They were able to make her presentable, and so it's an open casket," she said, grabbing my hand. She pulled me down a hallway, and I glanced back at Ransom, who began following us.

"Oh," I answered. "Well, um, that's good."

She squeezed my hand. "Most of the family is already here."

"Okay."

She led me through a small crowd of people to the casket, where her mom rested.

"She looks beautiful," I whispered, staring at the peaceful expression on Carol's face. She looked a lot like Remy, only not so rail-thin. Right now, Remy looked like she was twenty pounds underweight. With all of the stress in her life, I could certainly understand why. "Just like she's sleeping."

Remy reached over, and adjusted the necklace on Carol's dark blue dress. "I know. I keep waiting for her to open her eyes and tease me. Like she did when I was little. I'd go to her bedroom in the middle of the night, when I was scared, and stare at her until she woke up. She always seemed to know when I was there."

"I think she knows that you're here now, and is still watching you," I said softly.

She smiled sadly.

"Where's your fiancé?" I asked, looking around.

Her face darkened. "Taylor? Well, he had to stay another night. He's supposed to be here tomorrow, for the funeral."

"Oh. I'm sure he must feel awful."

She didn't say anything for a few seconds, and then lowered her voice. "The truth is, mom didn't care for Taylor that much, and I think he sensed it. They didn't get a long."

Ransom moved beside us. "That's because mom was always a good judge of character," he said quietly.

"Don't start," she said, her jaw clenched.

"Tell me I'm wrong."

Seeing the anger in Remy's eyes, I quickly changed change the subject. "So, how long are you staying in town, Rem?"

"I... I don't know," she said. "I guess someone needs to go through her things, and..." she reached into her pocket and grabbed another tissue, "figure things out," she said, swiping at fresh tears.

"Oh, honey, if you need any help at all, please let me know," I said, putting an arm around her.

"Thanks."

"I'll help, too," said Ransom.

She snorted. "Yeah, right. Like you helped when dad died?"

His face fell. "I offered to help. Mom refused to let me."

"That's because of *Icon*. She didn't want to impose on your career."

"What?"

She let out a ragged sigh. "Mom never wanted to cause you any stress or get in the way of your music. You were always her Superstar-can-do-no-wrong-son."

He raised his voice. "Get in the way of my career? He was my father, for Christ's sake. If she would have just said something…"

"Shush," she hissed as everyone turned towards them. "Don't cause a fucking scene. I know it's hard not being the center of attention, but this is about mom, not you."

"You're incredible," he said, gritting his teeth.

"And you're intolerable," she said, glaring at him.

He shook his head in disgust and walked away.

"Wow. Not much has changed between you two," I said.

She rubbed her forehead. "He just pisses me off so much sometimes. Always acting like a fucking baby."

"He *did* offer to help," I pointed out.

"I don't want his help. Besides, he'd probably be wasted the entire time, and be more of a pain in the ass than anything."

"Does he really drink that much?"

"Taylor says that Ransom is out of control, and doesn't care about anyone or anything."

"How does Taylor know about all of this?" I asked.

"He hears about everything. He's like a walking tabloid of information."

"Tabloid?"

"A lot of that stuff is true, you know," she said. "Just a little exaggerated."

"That's what I keep hearing, but I still find it hard to believe that these tabloids know what's going on behind closed doors."

"Oh, they have their ways," she said. "Anyway, Taylor says that it's pretty common knowledge in Hollywood that Ransom is into a lot of things; not just booze and women."

I stared at her in shock. "You think he's doing drugs?"

"Taylor said he is," she answered as we walked away from the casket.

"Has he actually seen him do drugs?"

She opened up her purse and pulled out a pack of cigarettes. "He doesn't have to. Like I said, he hears *everything*, and has connections all over town. Look, Ransom is a heavy-duty partier, and the only thing he has going for him, is his agent, who keeps him in line. Taylor said that he was even late for Icon the other day, and didn't give a shit. Hell, he almost got kicked off the show. Talk about pathetic! I mean the guy is making millions, and it's all due to Icon."

"Well, I'm sorry to hear that," I told her. "Have you tried talking to him about it?"

"I've mentioned it, but he denies the drugs."

"And you still don't believe him?"

She shrugged. "I don't know. Obviously, he has a problem with booze. Why would drugs be so hard to believe?"

"That's too bad," I said, scanning the room for Ransom, who was nowhere in sight.

"Enough about him. I'm going to have a smoke, and make some phone calls. There's a buffet set up downstairs, if you're hungry."

"Thanks," I said, although I'd lost my appetite.

She kissed my cheek. "Thanks again for coming, hon. If you can't stick around, I understand."

"No, I can stay, for as long as you need me."

"Thanks. I'll find you in a little while. Go check out the food," she said, walking away.

I wasn't sure what to do. Besides Ransom, I didn't know anyone else and I wasn't interested in eating. Wondering if he was really doing okay, I decided to go in search of him.

I left the viewing area and went downstairs to the lower level of the funeral home. Noticing he wasn't near the buffet table, which was currently being raided by a bunch of young kids, I wandered down another hallway, until I found him sitting alone, in what appeared to be some kind of waiting room. As I drew closer, I noticed him sipping from a small brown bag, and staring silently into space.

"Hi," I said, stopping in the doorway.

He looked up from the sofa he was on, and grinned. "Hi yourself."

I walked inside and crossed my arms under my chest. "What are you doing in here?"

"Oh… just easing the pain a little," he said, holding up the bottle. "You want some?"

"No, thank you."

He took a swig. "Suit yourself."

I nodded towards the bottle. "So, is it helping?"

He smiled humorlessly. "No, not really. But, it seems to be my best friend these days."

I sat down next to him on the flowered sofa, which was as hard as a rock. "So, what's your poison?"

"Tequila," he replied, taking another swig.

"Ah. I drank tequila once."

He wiped his mouth. "Only once?"

"Yes. I was nineteen, obviously, underage. I went to a party with some of the girls from my Cosmetology school." I sat back and chuckled, remembering how I'd slept next to the toilet, vowing to never touch another ounce of alcohol as long as I lived. "We all got so wasted, I think I lost five pounds the next day, I threw up so much."

"Funny, tequila never gets me sick. Well, unless I mix it with other booze. I've learned to just stick with what I know."

"What do you mean?"

"Tequila with a splash of soda. We know each other well."

I looked at the bottle. "With a splash? You seemed to have forgotten your splash today."

He chuckled, that low rumbly sound that always made me smile. "Guess so."

I sighed. "Are you okay?"

Ransom looked straight ahead. "Explain 'okay'."

I reached over and touched his arm. Even now he was so tense. "Are you handling all of this?"

Relaxing slightly, he stared at my fingers and smirked. "I knew you couldn't keep your hands off of me."

I quickly removed it. "Changing the subject?"

He grabbed my hand and put it back on his arm. "Only if you stop touching me."

I stared at him, not knowing what to say.

"I've been thinking about you a lot the last few days," he said, licking his lips. "Even with mom's death and all."

"Oh?" I whispered, wondering what exactly he'd been thinking.

He touched my cheek. "There's something so... refreshing about you. So... good and clean."

I laughed nervously. "It could just be the cucumber melon shower gel. It is pretty refreshing."

His face broke into a wide grin.

I smiled back. "Or –"

Before I could finish, he lowered his mouth to mine, his lips even softer than I'd remembered.

Sighing in pleasure, I closed my eyes and slid my hand behind his neck, pulling him closer. His tongue slid into my mouth and I greeted it with enthusiasm.

Tequila had never tasted so good.

I knew without a doubt that I still had it bad for this guy. I'd never met anyone who'd taken my breath away or made my heart skip so many beats. Then there were the butterflies in my stomach, all racing with excitement. I wondered if God would forgive me for feeling this happy during such a morbid time.

"What the fuck is going on in here?"

We broke away and stared at Remy guiltily, who was glowering at both of us in the doorway.

"Don't you know how to knock?" asked Ransom.

"The door is open," she replied, stepping inside. "God, Ransom, isn't it enough that you have to fuck every willing fan within miles, but now you just have to take advantage of one of my dearest friends?"

He stood up. "I wasn't taking advantage of Tiffany. Anyway, why don't you mind your own business? This has nothing to do with you."

She glared at him. "You should be ashamed of yourself. Drinking at mom's wake, and fucking with Tiffany's mind, and God knows what else?" she said, turning towards me. "Don't let him use you like this. Not only is he just out for a piece of ass, he wants you off of Icon. He said he'd do whatever it takes to get you off of the show, and obviously, it includes seduction."

My cheeks turned red. I stood up. "I... this..."

"Shut up, Remy," ordered Ransom. "That has nothing to do with this. Quit trying to confuse the hell out of her."

I turned back to him. "You're really seriously trying to get me off of the show? But why?"

Before he could answer, Remy spoke up.

"That is a good question, and, obviously, he'll stop at nothing to do it," she said, putting her hands on her hips. "Hell, it's only obvious that it was Ransom who called the media to let them know he was getting his hair cut at your salon the other day. Seriously, what do you think would happen if Icon found out about it? He's a judge and you're a contestant. I doubt they'd let that slide."

I stared at Ransom in disbelief. "You called the reporters?"

"No, of course not," he replied angrily. "I had nothing to do with that."

"Oh, come on! How else would they have found out, Tiff?" asked Remy. "Did Ransom make an appointment?"

"No," I said, staring at the wall. "He didn't."

"Well, there you go. Someone tipped them off! He already told me that he wants you off of Icon. He chose your salon when he already has a hair designer that will cut his hair whenever needed. The media show up on *that* day, at *that* hour. Coincidence?"

My eyes filled with tears. She had to be right. There was no other way they could have found out about it.

"Why are you being such a bitch?" asked Ransom.

"Why are *you* doing this to Tiffany?" she bit back. "You should be rooting for her!"

He turned back to me. "I didn't call the media. I ran out the back door. Why would I do that if I wanted to be seen with you?"

"Hello? To look innocent!" she hollered.

I didn't know who or what to believe, anymore. If Ransom was really trying to get me kicked off of the show, then it also meant his kisses were all part of the act. "Look, I have to go," I said, grabbing my purse from the sofa. "I'll see you both tomorrow at the funeral."

"Wait," said Ransom as I moved towards the door. He grabbed my arm. "Don't leave yet. Please. We need to talk."

"I'm sorry," I said, avoiding his eyes. "I should really get home. I... I have laundry to do."

"Let her go," said Remy. "You've confused her enough."

"I swear, I didn't call those reporters," he said, touching my cheek. "You have to believe me."

Remy pulled me away from him. "Leave her alone, big brother. Go back to your bottle. Besides music, it's the only other thing you're good at."

"Why are you such a cold-hearted bitch?" he asked.

She smiled coldly. "Why are you such a lying prick?"

I backed away from both of them. "Sorry, I have to go. I'll see you at the funeral tomorrow." Then, before either of them could say respond, I left.

Chapter Sixteen

Ransom

After Tiffany left, I was so pissed off at Remy, I wanted to throttle her.

"Good going," I snapped, grabbing my bottle from the end table. "Now she thinks I'm lying."

"Oh, and you're not?" she asked, folding her arms under her chest.

I glared at her. "No. For your information, I had nothing to do with that. Yeah, fine, I did go to the salon to try and talk her out of the contest, but I did *not* call the press."

Her cell phone started ringing. She pulled it out of her purse, and stared at the phone. "It's Taylor again. Look, just leave Tiffany alone, Ransom. You have no business putting the moves on my best friend. I won't have you hurting her."

"I'm not out to hurt her," I said, gritting my teeth.

"Christ, Ransom, face it, you hurt everyone. It's in your nature," she replied before answering the phone.

"This is bullshit," I mumbled. "I'm outta here."

She glared at me as I stepped around her, and pulled out my own phone. I dialed Tiffany, but she didn't answer.

"Fuck."

From the look in her eyes, it was obvious she still believed that I'd called the reporters. The thought of her thinking that I deceived her made me sick to my stomach. I needed to set her straight.

I shoved the bottle of tequila into my waistband, walked back to the viewing room, and pulled one of my cousins, Scott, aside.

"Can you give me a lift somewhere?" I asked the young eighteen-year-old. I hadn't seen him in three years. Now he was ripped, sported a crew cut, and there was talk of him entering the Army.

He stared at me in surprise, and then nodded solemnly. "Of course, man. Hey, I'm sorry for your loss."

"Thanks."

"I loved Aunt Carol," he said. "She made the best strawberry cheesecake and apple pies."

I smiled. "That she did."

He waved his hand towards the other guests. "Don't you need to stick around?"

I noticed Remy stepping back into the room, and shook my head. "No. It's getting too crowded in here. I need some fresh air."

He looked over at my sister, who was scowling at us. It wasn't a secret that Remy had a temper and liked to boss the cousins around, along with her older brother. "I hear that. Well, whenever you're ready."

Remy started walking towards us.

"Now is good," I replied, pulling him the other way.

***

It was just after ten o'clock by the time we pulled up to Tiffany's apartment building. Instead of heading to her place directly from the funeral home, we'd driven around town, talking about the family, and the good old days.

As we parked, I pulled out the brown bag and took a generous swig.

Liquid courage.

"Hey, can I have a drink?" asked Scott.

I frowned. "You're not legal."

"Come on, were you legal when you started?"

I wasn't, but there was no way I'd divulge that information to my young, impressionable cousin. One set on getting into the military. "We're talking about you, not me. Besides, you shouldn't drink and drive."

He tapped his thumbs on the steering wheel. "I do it all the time, man. I can handle it. Just a swig?"

"Nah, but here," I said, pulling out my wallet. I handed him a hundred dollar bill. "Go buy yourself a burger or taco somewhere."

His face lit up. "Thanks, man."

"No problem. Least I can do."

He pulled out his wallet and stuck the bill inside. "What's it like being a super-star,

Ransom? You must have chicks throwing themselves at you night and day."

That's the first question guys always asked me – how much ass was I getting? I chuckled. "You could say that."

"I wish I had your life."

"It's not all it's cracked up to be."

His eyebrows shot up. "What do you mean?"

"Sorry, bud, I don't have time to explain it right now. Just be thankful of what you have, and never sell out for anything."

"Sell out?"

I turned my head and belched. "Sorry. What I mean is, always read the small print."

"Oh. So, I thought you'd have a big mansion in Beverly Hills," he said, nodding towards the apartment building.

"I don't live here, but I don't live in Beverly Hills either," I said, opening the car door.

He put his arm on the seat and stared up at me as I got out. "So, where's your home then?"

I smirked. "Where the heart is. Unfortunately, I've been told I don't have one."

He chuckled. "Oh, hell. You don't need one. You're Ransom. People will love you no matter what."

I wasn't so sure about that. Whoever murdered my mother may have been someone who really hated me. She was one of the sweetest women alive, and I couldn't imagine someone shooting her randomly. "Go eat or call one of your girlfriends up," I told him. "Just stay away from drinking. It'll get you into trouble."

He stared at the bag in my hand. "Right."

I looked down at the bag guiltily. "I suppose I should practice what I preach."

"No, man, it's cool. It's what you do. Everyone knows that."

I stood up straight. "I'll catch ya later, Scott. Drive safely."

"You too, man."

I closed the door and watched as he left the parking lot. Then I walked over to the garbage dumpster and threw the bottle away, wincing at the loud noise that echoed in the darkness. Swearing under my breath, I walked to Tiffany's building, stepped into the lobby, and buzzed her apartment. Unfortunately, she didn't answer.

Fuck.

I stepped back outside and glanced up at the top apartment on the left.

Her light was on.

I smiled. *Bingo.*

Quietly, I stepped over to the private patio two floors below, and then hoisted myself to the second floor deck and kept going until I was on her deck, grateful that the sound of the air conditioning units blocked most of the noise. I then pulled out my phone, and sent her a text, informing her that I was on her balcony.

Ten seconds later, her light went out and the glass door slid open. "What in the hell are you doing?" she whispered, glaring at me angrily.

I stared down at her and got an immediate hard-on. She had on a short, white, sleeveless nightgown that was decorated with tiny hearts, and it was more than obvious that she was braless. Her nipples hardened under my gaze and she folded her arms across her chest.

"You weren't answering my calls," I whispered back.

She scowled. "I was sleeping."

I smirked. "With the lights on?"

She rolled her eyes. "*What* do you want?"

I nodded towards her apartment. "Can we talk inside? Someone might notice me."

She immediately opened the door and stepped back.

Biting back another smile, I stepped into her living room and watched as she shut the door.

"Is that what you sleep in?"

She looked down. "Um, yes. I'm going to put on a robe. I'll be right back."

I grabbed her arm before she could walk away. "Slow down there. This won't take long."

"*What* won't take long?"

I'd come to explain myself. To tell her that she was too good for Icon. That there were other ways for her to start a singing career. That once they had her in their claws, they'd own her soul, and she'd be miserable like me. But instead, all I could do was stare down into her blue eyes and wade in their depths. "Do you believe me? About the reporters?"

"I don't know, I mean I *want* to believe you wouldn't be that horrible."

"I swear to God, I didn't call them. I wouldn't sink that low. I wouldn't do that to you."

She stared up at me, searching my eyes for the truth. "I sincerely hope not."

Chapter Seventeen

Tiffany

My heart was pounding in my chest as he stared at my lips. I thought about the earlier kiss, and a felt a warm flutter of excitement in my lower stomach.

He began unbuttoning his suit jacket.

"Uh, what are you doing?" I asked. "It's late, you should really get going home, don't you think?"

"I *think* it's time you stop trying to get rid of me," he replied, dropping his jacket onto my sofa. "We both know that it's not what you really want."

"Is that right?" I asked, staring in surprise as he removed his tie. "You think I want you here?"

He took a step closer and smiled arrogantly. "Tell me I'm wrong."

"You –"

Before I could continue, he had his arms around my waist, and was pressing me against the wall, his mouth on mine. "God, you smell so good, and I want you so fucking much," he whispered, moving to my neck. "I can't stop thinking about you."

My legs turned to jelly as his lips made a warm, shivery trail from my neck, back to my mouth. I closed my eyes, and kissed him back hungrily, not caring about anything else but his tongue in my mouth.

His left hand slid under my nightgown, over my ribcage, to my breast. He groaned in the back of his throat as he squeezed, and then sought out my nipple with his fingers, sending a flare of heat to the junction between my legs. He pinched and rolled the tip as his other hand slid to my bottom, pressing me against the hard bulge in his pants, driving me crazy. I wanted to crawl on top of him, wrap my legs around his hips, and feel him inside of me.

Breathing harder, he raised my nightgown, exposing my breast, and replaced his fingers with his warm, wet tongue.

"Oh..," I moaned, bringing my hand to his zipper, frantic to touch him as he devoured my right breast with his mouth, licking and teasing the hard tip. Closing my eyes, I touched the outline of his erection, imagining its fullness sliding into me, in and out.

He sucked in his breath as I began stroking him through the fabric, unable to help myself. "You'd better tell me now if you want to stop," he groaned.

In answer, I unbuttoned his pants, slid my hand into his boxers, and wrapped my hand around the prize.

And what a prize it was.

Before I could get a closer look, he lifted me up in the air, wrapped my legs around his waist, and carried me towards the bedroom.

"I take it you're all right with this?" he asked with a sexy smile as he lowered me to the mattress.

I was beyond ready.

I grabbed his neck, pulled his mouth back to mine, and wrapped my legs around his hips to show him.

He slid his hands around my rear, cupping both cheeks. His mouth moved from my lips to my ear. "I want to taste all of you," he whispered, his hand moving down my stomach to my panties.

I held my breath as he trailed a finger to the cleft between my legs and stopped.

He groaned. "Fuck, you're so wet for me." Then his fingers began to strum the outside of my panties.

I moaned as his fingers moved faster, and then stopped. He pushed the side of my panties over, touching my slicken clitoris with his index finger, and began rubbing the knot.

"Yeah," I gasped as he stroked and stroked, making me feel like I was going to come out of my skin.

He lowered his mouth to my left nipple, sucking the tip and then slid his finger deep inside.

"Please," I begged, my pelvis grinding against his fingers as he worked me over. "Ransom, please fuck me."

He removed his mouth from my breast, grabbed my panties with both hands, and tore them off of me.

"Say that again," he whispered, touching and stroking my sweet spot again.

I moaned. "Ransom, fuck me."

He smiled wickedly. "First I want me some Taffy."

I giggled but it turned into a gasp of pleasure as he spread my thighs apart, and buried his face there. I raised my hands above my head and grabbed the edge of the bed to hold on as his mouth began to torment me in the sweetest ways possible. Just when I thought it couldn't feel any more fantastic, he slid two fingers inside, and began to move in sync with his relentless tongue. I grabbed the top of his hair, and within seconds, felt my hips begin to buck right before a final few flicks sent me over the edge. Screaming out loud, I tensed up and shuddered in ecstasy as I rode out the orgasm, which was longer, and more intense than anything I'd ever remembered.

He sat up and wiped his mouth with the back of his hand. "Fuck, was that sexy."

Breathless, I could only smile, my legs still trembling.

Staring down at me, he unbuttoned his shirt, and tossed it to the floor. Then I watched in anticipation as he stood up, removed his pants, and then finally, his boxers. When he was completely naked, I had to wonder who was luckier – me, because I was going to have sex with the man of my dreams, or Ransom himself, because of all that he'd been handed in life. Not only did he have an amazing voice, but naked, he was hard and thick in all the right places.

"Are you for real?" I whispered, staring at his shaft in delight.

He chuckled and shook his head. "I hope you mean that in a good way."

"Oh, yeah."

His shoulders were broad, his waist was narrow, and it all led to a package that was more than I'd anticipated.

He crawled back onto the bed and nudged my opening with the tip of his cock before his lips sought mine.

I reached my hand below, circling his erection, and he groaned into my mouth. It made me feel powerful.

I pushed him onto his back, and he stared up at me, his eyes smoldering with desire.

"My turn," I whispered, sliding my hand round his shaft.

"Tiffany," he gasped, as I took him in my mouth, licking the moisture at the top.

"Wait," he whispered hoarsely, pulling away after a few bobs of my head. "I don't want to come yet." Then he had me on my back, my legs spread apart. He rubbed the tip of his shaft against my opening, sliding it down and back up, tormenting me. It felt so good but it wasn't enough; I needed to feel him inside of me. I spread my legs wider, trying to draw him in.

"Wait," he whispered. "We need a condom." He reached down to the floor, grabbed his wallet, and took one out. Once it was on, he rubbed my entrance with the tip of his cock and then plunged inside.

I moaned as his hips pulled back, and then he thrust again, this time harder.

"Fuck, this feels so good," he said, thrusting again, the tight, slick contact making the veins in his neck and shoulder bulge with restraint. Soon, his thrusts grew stronger, deeper, and longer, making me moan in sheer pleasure.

Staring up at him as he continued to plow into me, I felt another orgasm beginning to build, eager and urgent for release.

***

Ransom

I stared down at Tiffany, trying not to come before she did, but it was harder than hell to keep any kind of control, especially with a woman as sexy as her. With her full breasts and hard nipples pointing up towards me, I had an incredible urge to pull out and rub myself against them, but the tightness between her legs was too fucking good to leave. Instead, I kept moving in and out of her, memorizing every detail of her face as she stared up at me.

Damn, she was so beautiful.

It was how I'd imagined it, only better. Her blonde hair was spread across the pillow, her eyes staring up at me, as she moaned. I'd already made her come once, and the hell if I was going to do it until she experienced another. This girl had wanted me, back when I was just an average teenager. Now I was a man and I wanted her to feel like a woman.

"Ransom," she moaned again, arching her back. Crying out, she dug her nails into my hips, and locked onto my cock with her pelvic muscles, sending *me* over the edge as she reached her climax.

I groaned in pleasure, feeling as if she was somehow massaging me down below. With a final thrust, I exploded inside of her while she wrapped her legs around my waist again, not letting me go. As I grew soft, I stared down at Tiffany and felt a sudden urge to hold her in my arms, and not let her go. It wasn't a feeling that I was used to.

Swallowing, I removed the condom, tossed it into the garbage next to her bed, and then pulled her close. Smiling, I shut my eyes and sighed.

"Are you okay?"

"I am more than okay," I whispered, kissing the top of her head. "How about you?"

She smiled up at me. "I'm... fabulous."

"Good," I replied, still grinning with the realization that for the first time in a very long while, I was somewhere that I wanted to be.

And I was completely sober.

Chapter Eighteen

Tiffany

I opened my eyes the next morning and sat up quickly, images from the night before flashing in my head.

Ransom.

Looking around the bedroom, I sighed with relief. His clothes were still on the floor. He hadn't bolted, and I hoped it was a sign that he didn't regret what had happened.

I grabbed a short, pink terrycloth robe, and walked out to the kitchen, where he stood in his boxers, bent down, and searching inside of my refrigerator.

"What are you doing?" I asked, coming up behind him.

"Well, I was going to surprise you with breakfast, but your refrigerator is empty, Taffy," he said, standing up.

I moved around him and looked inside. I smiled. "What, you don't like yogurt, turkey bacon, or bran muffins?"

"Sorry, I hate Greek yogurt, turkey bacon has no taste, and bran muffins are for old codgers who need to poop."

I laughed.

He walked over to my cupboards, and began opening doors. "Do you have any pancake mix or the fixings for French toast?"

"Sorry, no. It's just me and I hardly have time to eat. Plus, I have to watch my figure."

He looked at me and smiled. "Watch your figure?" He walked back over to me and tugged at the belt on my robe, opening it. "I'll watch it," he said, his voice husky as his eyes traveled over my nakedness. His teeth grazed his lower lip as his hands slid over my hips, pulling me against him. "That way you can eat what you want."

I smiled as his lips touched my collarbone, and one of his hands cupped my breast. I remembered the incredible orgasms he'd given me the night before, and felt a tingle between my legs. "You're crazy, you know that?"

"That's what they say," he whispered between nibbles on my neck, "But I don't recall ever being this crazy before. In fact, I think I'd like to get even crazier by finding new ways to make you scream."

My cheeks turned red. "Sorry, I guess I was a little loud."

He bit my ear, making me shiver. "I loved it," he murmured, tightening his grip on my backside. "Hell, I'm harder than a rock just thinking about you screaming."

"Then quit thinking about it," I whispered back, sliding my hand down his boxers. All of this talk was making me incredibly hungry, and yogurt was the last thing on my mind.

With a grunt of pleasure, he picked me up, and carried me back into the bedroom where he did find a few new ways to make me scream.

***

After a few more rounds in Tiffany's bed, we both took showers, and then went out for lunch at Zeke's, a local diner. Fortunately, it was after two o'clock in the afternoon, so there weren't too many people in the restaurant.

"What time is the funeral again?" I asked as I dipped my fry into a cup of seasoned sour cream, and stuffed it into my mouth.

She looked up at me from her salad, her blue eyes larger than life. Her hair was still damp, her face void of makeup, and she was so beautiful that all I could think about was getting her back into bed. "You're asking *me*?"

"I think I shot out most of my brain cells that last round," I replied, smiling wickedly.

The truth was that I'd been in a state of fugue before the wake. If it hadn't been for Sonia dropping me off at the funeral home the night before, I would have probably missed that as well. All I'd thought about was my mother, and the horror she must have felt staring at the barrel of the gun that shot her. Disturbing images of her frightened face as she realized what was happening had haunted me all week. Then, last night, being with Tiffany had taken me away from the cold harsh truth of reality for a short time. Now I wanted more. Much more. She was like a drug, a very addictive one.

She blushed, and it actually brought a tug of pleasure in my chest. "Well, the funeral is at five o'clock. I'm sure you'll want to be there before it starts."

What I wanted was to grab Tiffany, charter a plane, and get lost in a place where nobody could find us. Just the two of us, and a bed. "I suppose. You're going, right?"

"Of course I'm going."

"Good." I reached over and grabbed her hand. "I don't think I'd want to go if you weren't there."

"As flattering as that sounds, you'd have to go even if I couldn't make it. Your mom would turn over in her grave if you didn't show."

I sighed and looked out the window. "I know. I'm just not looking forward to this big fiasco that's taking place tonight."

She took a drink of water. "I thought it was going to be a private funeral."

"It's supposed to be, but most of these people are strangers to me and Remy. Mom only had a handful of friends when we were growing up." I smiled wryly. "I'm pretty certain that the newer ones are quite aware of who her son is. Just like my father's funeral, they'll come to get a glimpse of me. It's pretty pathetic."

Her eyes softened. "Don't let it bother you. Just focus on being there for her, remembering her, and paying *your* respects."

Our eyes met. "You're right. I'm sure Sonia has set up enough security, that even my mom will be scrutinized."

She made that cute snorting noise again, and I bit my lip, wishing we were alone. I couldn't get enough of her. Her laugh, her smile, her body underneath mine...

"Excuse me," asked our waitress, a young woman who'd done a double-take when she'd originally greeted us. "I'm sorry to be nosy, but are you that singer, *Ransom*?"

"No," I answered, smiling broadly. "But don't tell *her* that." I nodded towards Tiffany. "It's how I talked her into joining me for lunch."

The waitress laughed. "Oh... sorry, I guess I blew your cover then."

"It's not a problem," replied Tiffany, her eyes sparkling. "From what I hear, the *real* Ransom is quite the player, and would be at lunch with a group of five or six girls. He probably thinks the word *monogamous* is some kind of bad cough."

"True," replied the waitress. "And I doubt he'd be in this dive. Would either of you like a refill on your water or soda?"

"Just more water," I said.

"Me too," replied Tiffany.

When the waitress walked away I stared at her. "That was really harsh. 'The *real* Ransom doesn't know how to be monogamous'?"

"Oh, hell," replied Tiffany, with a chuckle. "Don't even try telling me otherwise."

"I can be monogamous," I protested.

She tilted her head. "Right. You know, last night and this morning was *incredible*, but, honestly, I don't expect *anything* from you. I want you to know that."

I reached over and grabbed her hand. "I want *you* to know something. Last night was special for me, too. It meant a lot. Yes, I've had a lot of women go through my life these last couple of years. Too many. In fact, if you want to know the truth, it's been one big blur. Most of them, hell, I don't even remember their names."

"Nice," she replied, smiling. "I'm glad we used protection."

I rubbed the top of her hand with my thumb. "Don't worry, honey, I *always* use protection."

"Always?"

"Yes. As drunk as I've gotten, I have never blacked out. So you see, I *always* use a condom to protect myself. That is," I chuckled and lowered my voice, "when I can actually perform."

Her jaw dropped. "What?"

"Hey, I'm not afraid to admit that easy or slutty chicks don't do it for me. Not anymore. Not like when I was in my early twenties and just wanted to wax my dick every chance I'd get."

She shook her head. "Wow. I am just... wow. Seriously, wax your dick? That sounds gross, even coming from you."

"Sorry," I said, kissing the side of her hand. "Basically, what I'm saying is that I've been thinking a lot about you. You're like a breath of fresh air, Taffy. Not only do I have a lot of respect for you, but you're so damn real. You're not fake, not like most of the women I've met who are only interested in me because... well, obviously because I'm famous."

She arched an eyebrow. "How do you know that *I'm* not after you for your money or your fame?"

I chuckled and released her hand. "Because you're only after me for my body."

She smirked. "Is that right?"

I grabbed another fry. "Don't deny it. You know, I haven't forgotten that kiss, at my graduation party."

"I was just a kid," she replied, picking up a cucumber with her fork. She brought it to her lips, and something about the way she licked the white dressing from the corner of her mouth made my pants tighten.

"You're definitely not anymore."

She smiled. "At least you were man enough to push me away. Although, it hurt when you did that, though, you know."

"I'm sorry," I replied. "I didn't want to, but I had to. You were much too young."

"I'm glad that you did it, because," she grabbed a cherry tomato with her fork. "It now makes me respect you that much more."

I watched her slip the tomato into her mouth. "You respect me?"

She finished chewing, and nodded. "Of course. You're a good man, Ransom. I know we haven't spent a lot of time together, and most of what I do know of you these days is from the tabloids, but I can tell you still have a decent side to you."

"I'll take that as a compliment," I replied, sticking another fry into my mouth.

"I mean, you could work on your table manners," she teased. "Like closing your mouth when you eat, but other than that, you're a pretty good guy."

I opened my mouth and stuck out my tongue.

She rolled her eyes. "Okay, that's gross."

I leaned forward. "That's not what you were saying earlier when my tongue was out."

Her face turned red, and I smiled.

We finished the rest of our food in silence, and when I finished the rest of my burger, she looked at her watch. "Do you need a lift anywhere before the funeral?"

I looked down at my clothes. "I need a new suit. Can we stop at my place?"

"Your place?"

"Yeah."

She bit her lower lip. "I don't want anyone to see us together. What if Icon finds out?"

I stared at her incredulously. "Icon? You're still going through with the contest? After everything that's happened?"

"Well, yeah, why?"

I sat up straighter. "I thought you'd come to your senses after my mom's murder, and what happened between us last night."

"What are you talking about?" she asked, frowning.

"It's what I've been trying to tell you all along. This contest is a mistake. Seriously, you have no idea what it's like, once you've signed the dotted line with Icon. It seems like the American dream, but it's far from it."

She frowned. "How can a television contest seriously be that bad? One that made you a star. A very rich and successful one at that."

"Sure, it all looks awesome from the outside." People at the next table turned to stare at us, and I lowered my voice. "But, Icon is a cesspool of greedy assholes who will give you a record contract with a lot of glam, but take away most of your freedom in return."

"Explain what you mean by that," she said, looking at me like I was nuts. "You seem pretty free to me."

"That's how it looks, but believe me, I'm far from being free. Hell, being here without their permission is against my contract. Sleeping somewhere in a place where they can't monitor me, *isn't* part of the contract. I can't even take a shit without them knowing where it is, or what brand of toilet paper I'm using, because of the damn contract. Is that what you really want?"

She shrugged. "Maybe you should have negotiated a better contract."

"They don't negotiate," I said matter-of-factly.

"You know for sure?" she asked, her eyes searching mine.

No, I didn't know for sure, but I wasn't going to admit it. If she actually won the contest, she'd probably be too enamored with the prizes to question what was in the small print. I knew Taffy, and I also knew how manipulative Icon was. "Yes," I lied. "There is no negotiating. It's all or nothing."

She put her salad fork down. "Well, regardless, Ransom, I'm not some gullible little ninny who can't read a contract, or make her own decisions. I mean, you're kind of jumping the gun anyway. I probably won't even make it past the second round."

"I'm not saying you're gullible. I'm saying that it's a lot of work to make it that far, possibly go all the way, only to have them dictate your life for the next seven years. It's not worth it."

"I'd like to be the judge of that. You've made it, and aren't happy," she said, staring at me angrily. "I see that. But you are not me, and I should be able to make my own decisions."

"That's the same way I felt at your age, but when it comes to this show, you definitely need someone to point you in the right direction, and that person is me."

"You're not pointing me anywhere; you're just pushing me away from success."

"Hey, I want you to be successful," I said. "But there are other ways..."

She groaned. "Look, I appreciate your concern, but if you're not going to support or root for me, then, well, get out of the way, because I'm *not* giving up on this contest. I'm *going* to the next round," she said, her eyes hard. "I need to do this, Ransom. It's what I've always dreamed of."

I opened my mouth to tell her that the dream she had shouldn't be signing with Icon, and that I'd help her get into the music industry if she really wanted to, but then our waitress returned.

"Would either of you care for dessert?" she asked, staring at me curiously. I wondered how much she'd actually heard and looked towards Tiffany.

"No," replied Tiffany, looking down at her leftovers. "In fact, I'm no longer hungry. Can you please bring us the tab?"

"Sure thing," she said, taking the bill out of her apron. "You can pay at the register. Have a good night, and come back real soon."

"Thanks," said Taffy, grabbing the tab.

"Hey, I've got it," I said, trying to take the bill from her as the waitress left.

"No," she said. "*I'm* paying for it. I'd hate to make you spend money that you made from Icon, on *this* food, knowing how much it bothers you."

Frustrated, I grabbed her wrist, and leaned forward. "I made the money *for* Icon. *My* voice made them millions of dollars."

She snaked her hand away. "Good for you, and good for them. Look, I have a headache and just want to lie down before the funeral. Can you call your drivers, and have them come and get you?"

I sighed. "Tiffany –"

She scooted out of the booth. "Thanks. I'll see you tonight at the funeral."

"Look, I'm sorry if you're upset. I'm just trying to help you."

"Save it," she said. "I'm seriously tired of arguing."

I stood up and watched as she grabbed her purse, and then stormed out of the diner.

Chapter Nineteen

Tiffany

I was so angry when I left the diner, that I barely remembered driving back to my apartment. It wasn't until I threw my purse on the sofa and sank down into my chaise that I realized I'd abandoned a famous celebrity like Ransom in an old, dumpy diner. Stifling a giggle, I closed my eyes and began rubbing my temples. As my headache began to subside, my phone vibrated.

A message.

I grabbed my purse and checked the message. It was from Ransom.

Are you okay?

Yes, I answered. *Just a headache.*

Do you feel better now that you left your headache at Zeke's?

I laughed. *Sorry. Did you find a ride?*

Yes.

Well, I'll see you in a couple hours.

I hope so.

You will. I'd never miss your mom's funeral. I already miss you.

Feeling a pang of pleasure in my chest, I smiled. *You're such a flirt.*

Not flirting. Dead serious. Can I give you a ride to the funeral?

I hesitated, knowing that the media would be close enough to possibly snap a picture of us together. *No, I can drive.*

He paused for a few seconds. *No, I'll pick you up. I know what you're worried about, and I promise, nobody will know if we play it cool at the funeral. We don't even have to sit together.*

Fine.

I'll pick you up in the lobby at four-thirty.

Okay.

He didn't send another text, so I put my phone on the charger. As I walked away, it went off.

I picked it up and cringed, ready for the tongue lashing. "Hi, Remy."

"What's going on between you and Ransom?"

I smirked. "Well, you certainly don't mess around."

She sighed. "I'm worried about you, Tiffany. He's a womanizer, a drunk, and not somebody you want to get involved with. Hell, he's a fucking mess."

"Oh, come on. He's not *that* bad."

"Yes, he is. You have no idea how fucked up he is. Just stay away from him. For your sake, for my sake. I don't want to lose you as a friend."

"You would never do that."

"Just, please, keep your distance from my brother. I know him a lot better than you do, Tiff."

"That's going to be a little hard since he's giving me a ride to the funeral."

She coughed. "No, absolutely not. I'll pick you up."

"There's no need to."

"Yes, I am picking you up. Besides, you know you're not supposed to be near one of the Icon judges."

"I know – we're going to act like strangers when we arrive. Besides, I probably shouldn't be around you either. You *are* one of the judge's sisters."

She sighed in frustration. "Fine, I'll send a limo for you. It's better than driving with Ransom. They'll still see you together, for sure."

I made my own decision. "Look, I'll just drive myself. I'll be there at five, sharp."

"Okay. Just do yourself a favor, Tiffany, and stay away from Ransom. He's no good for you or your music career. I know he bitches and complains about Icon, but seriously, I think you have an excellent shot at going all the way."

I smiled. "Do you *really* think so?"

"I really do. You know, your mom would be very proud of you. Hell, so would mine."

"I think our moms are still proud of both of us. Wherever they may be."

"I hope so. Anyway, just remember what I told you, and stay away from Ransom if you know what's good for you."

I bit the side of my nail. "I know you're right."

"I am. Listen, I have to go. I'll see you soon?"

"Okay."

She hung up, and I stared at the wall in the kitchen, wondering what I was going to do about Ransom. He was *so* persuasive, and saying "no" to a man like that wasn't easy. The fact that I couldn't stop thinking about him didn't help matters, either. I closed my eyes, picturing his hands and lips on my skin and released a frustrated sigh.

I already missed him, too.

I knew the timing wasn't right for us, but I couldn't help the way I felt. Not only did he drive me crazy in bed, but every time I pictured his smile, I felt all warm and fuzzy inside. The same way I'd felt as a teenager, only this time it was much more intense. If I wasn't careful, I'd let him talk me into shrugging away all of my plans for a singing career. But deep down, I knew that I'd never forgive myself if I walked away from the contest that easily. I had to see how far I could go. It's what my mother would have wanted.

Sighing, I decided to tell him the truth – that it was too risky to arrive at the service together. Heck, it was bad for both of us. No matter how much he disliked Icon, he was still under contract.

Making up my mind, I called and left him a message, telling Ransom that I'd see him at the funeral, but at a safe distance, and that if he wanted to talk, he could stop by my apartment later that evening.

He returned my call shortly, obviously frustrated. "This is ridiculous. I need you by my side. At least on the ride out there. It would mean a lot."

I closed my eyes, and pictured my mother's face, urging me to stay strong. That we didn't

even know each other that well, and he was
expecting too much from me. "Ransom, I just
can't take any chances," I pleaded.

He didn't say anything.

"I'm sorry about your mom, really I am.
But you're going to have so many people
surrounding you, people who love and support
you. And hell, I'll still be at the funeral, wishing
you the best."

"It's not the same thing," he replied, in a
clipped voice.

"Look, when the funeral is over, come back
to my place, and we'll talk."

He was quiet.

"Ransom?"

"Yeah."

"Just think about it, okay?"

"I'm leaving tomorrow afternoon. For New
York for more judging. After that, I'll be traveling
to the other locations, and won't be back for
another month or so."

"I understand," I said, feeling an emptiness
in the pit of my stomach. I was already missing
him, and he hadn't even left yet. This wasn't
good.

"Oh, fuck, I've got to go. Sonia's beating
down my door already."

"Okay," I replied. "I'll see you at the
funeral."

"Right."

"Goodbye."

He sighed. "Goodbye."

I hung up and leaned back against the wall, wondering if I was making a big mistake. My dream was to become a singer, a famous singer. But, was it worth pushing away the man I finally had... the one I'd also dreamed about?

Chapter Twenty

Ransom

Sonia was pissed off as all hell, and railed on me for an hour about being a douchebag.

"What the fuck? You didn't check in at all last night. Dammit, your mom was *murdered*, and nobody heard a peep out of you in the last twelve hours? I've left you several messages, which you didn't even have the decency to respond to!" she snapped, pacing back and forth. "You could have at least sent me a message, telling me you were still breathing!"

"Sorry," I replied, staring up at the ceiling as I lay back on my sofa. I'd turned off my phone again, knowing that it was the only way to keep anyone from hounding me. "I've had a lot of shit on my mind."

She sat down across from me on one of the leather club chairs. "I know, I get that, hon, but, you're giving me a fucking ulcer." She leaned forward and put her head in her hands. "I just can't do it anymore. I'm tired of babysitting. It's just too much work trying to get you to where you need to be, lying through my teeth to the studio about your whereabouts, and keeping your shit together for you. Dammit, Ransom," she looked over at me, "when are you just going to grow up?"

She just didn't get it.

"Sonia, I appreciate what you're trying to do, really. And I'm sorry for all of the trouble I've caused you, I really am, but the truth is – I want out. I *really* want out. After this season of Icon."

Her eyes bulged out of her head. "You want out?"

"Yeah. I'd like to hire a lawyer, one not associated with the show, and see if there is any way out of these fucking contracts."

She rubbed her forehead, and then nodded. "Fine, you want to leave Icon? There is a way, Ransom, but let me tell you, you will lose *everything. Everything.*"

I stared at her in surprise. "You're telling me that there is really a way out?"

She snorted. "You look surprised. Yes, there *always* was. But you'll lose the rights to all of your songs, and walk away without a dime."

I sat up. "The songs were theirs. They wrote them anyway."

"Well then, if you're okay with giving up your money, your homes, your cars, hell, that island you invested in... I'm talking *everything,* then, you can walk away. Hell, it's all in the contracts. I read them, didn't you?"

I grinned sheepishly.

"Skimmed them?" she replied with a snort. "Read only what you wanted to?"

"Hey, I was young and stupid. I didn't know anything back then."

"Obviously." She sighed. "Ransom, normally, I'd fight you on this, and tell you that you're making a big fucking mistake. A monstrous one. But, I've seen how miserable you are, and I know you have one hell of a voice, so

you'll recover. If this is really what you want, I'll
do what I can to help you."

"Even if you'll lose me for a client?"

Her eyes glinted. "I never said anything
about that. Those fuckers don't own *me*,
Ransom."

I raised my eyebrows. "I thought it was
Icon who hired you as my agent."

"They did," she said. "But unlike *you*, I
read the contracts, and negotiated before I signed
anything. I *never* read anything, anywhere that
indicated I couldn't represent you, should you
leave Icon, and believe me, I went over them
several dozen times."

I smiled. "You're good."

She put her feet up on the coffee table, and
grinned back. "Fucking-A-right, I am."

"I owe you."

"You've owed me for a long time now,
Ransom. You've just been too busy feeling sorry
for yourself to realize it."

"I'm finished with that. I'll do whatever I
can to pay you back."

"Good. One thing though, Ransom, I'm
going to have to insist that you stay sober while
we figure this thing out."

"No problem. Gladly."

"You need a ride to the funeral?" she
asked, checking her watch.

"You're going?"

She frowned. "Of course I'm going. Do you
think that I dressed up like this for shits and
giggles?"

I glanced down her black dress, and was reminded of how much she loathed wearing anything but pants. "You look nice."

"Thanks. I'm only doing it to pay my respects to your mom, God rest her soul." Her eyes softened. "You know, I only met her a few times, but I could tell she was a special woman."

I blinked back tears. "Yeah, she really was."

"Well, I'll let you get ready. Meet me in the lobby in an hour, and we'll take the limo."

"Okay."

"And, Ransom, remember what I told you, lay off of the booze. We need your head clear."

An image of Tiffany popped into my head, and I knew there was already one thing in my mind that was clear. I wouldn't leave Icon until she walked away first.

Chapter Twenty-One

Tiffany

After taking another shower, I slipped into a conservative black dress and heels, then pulled my hair back into a loose bun. Knowing I'd eventually look like a raccoon if I wore eye makeup to a funeral, I skipped the mascara, adding only a touch of lipstick. I topped it off with a spritz of perfume, stuffed a handful of tissue into my purse, and left my apartment.

It was a short drive to the funeral, which was in Glendale at Woodland Springs Baptist Church. Although it was a private service, the chapel was already packed by the time I arrived, which was twenty minutes before the service was to begin. Trying to remain inconspicuous, I sat in the back of the church, and read through the funeral program.

"Are you saving part of the bench for anyone?" asked a deep voice.

I looked up, and noticed a tall, blonde man standing at the end of the isle. I looked at the space next to me, which could probably seat three or four more people. "No, not at all."

"May I sit next to you?"

"Of course," I replied, moving over for him.

"Thank you," he said, sitting down. He pulled out the funeral pamphlet, and began reading it.

Just then, I noticed Ransom enter the large chapel from the west side of the church. His eyes scanned the crowd of people, and I wondered if he was looking for me.

"Did you know Carol well?" asked the man next to me.

I sighed. "Yes. I knew her fairly well. She was such a sweet lady."

"It's a shame. I hope they catch the person who did it."

"Yeah, me too."

"Her family must be just devastated."

"Yeah, they are."

"There are so many crazies out in the world. It just goes to show that you're not even safe in your own home these days."

"Guess not," I replied, turning away. I didn't mean to be rude, but I really wasn't in the mood for conversation.

Soon, organ music began to fill the chapel, and the funeral service began. Standing in the first two rows were Carol's family, including Ransom, Remy, and Taylor. Remy and Taylor were huddled close, while Ransom sat next to an older woman I didn't recognize, his face grim.

The service was heart-wrenching. Remy and her uncle each took turns up at the podium reminiscing about Carol, her incredible kindness towards others, and how much she loved her family. I smiled and shed tears through each of their stories. Then, Ransom was called up.

With his head held low, he walked to the front of the church, and took his place behind the podium. Like the others, there was a camera focused on his grief-stricken face, which appeared on a large white screen behind him.

"For my mother," he said in a husky voice. He glanced up at the congregation, and I could see the tears in his eyes. "Because, she used to hum it all the time when we were growing up." He smiled grimly. "Funny, it used to drive me nuts at the time, but now, I'd do anything to hear it again."

I leaned forward in anticipation, wondering what exactly he was going to sing. I also remembered Carol humming, and singing at their house, but I hadn't thought too much about it at the time.

He took a deep breath, cleared his throat, and began to sing.

Amazing grace,
How sweet the sound,
That saved a wretch like me,
I once was lost, but now am found,
Was blind, but now I see.

'Twas grace that taught my heart to fear,
And grace my fears relieved.
How precious did that grace appear
The hour I first believed.

Through many dangers, toils and snares
I have already come;
'Tis grace hath brought me safe thus far
And grace will lead me home.

The Lord has promised good to me
His word my hope secures;
He will my shield and portion be,
As long as life endures.

Yea, when this flesh and heart shall fail,
And mortal life shall cease,
I shall possess within the veil,
A life of joy and peace.

When we've been there ten thousand years
Bright shining as the sun,
We've no less days to sing God's praise
Than when we've first begun.

He stopped singing and the chapel was dead silent, except for a baby that started fussing.

"Love you, mom," he mumbled, brushing at his tear-streaked face.

The church erupted into a roar of applause, and he stepped away from the podium, his head now down.

I wiped my face, still shaken. I knew Ransom was talented; he hadn't gone all the way on Icon because of his personality, or charming smile. No, it was his singing that had won the hearts of America, along with his enthusiasm for the music, which he had plenty of, back in the earlier part of his career. Over time, I, along with the rest of his fans, had noticed that his excitement and passion had begun to wane, especially recently. This ballad was a reminder of why he'd become such a superstar to begin with. There was nothing in the world like his voice.

Nothing.

I closed my eyes and sighed. The rich timbre of his voice and the raw emotion in his eyes had touched me deeply. I actually felt ashamed for not standing by his side when *he* needed me the most. Now, I wanted to throw my arms around him, tell him how beautiful it was, and that his mother was surely staring down at him with loving pride.

"Wow," whispered the man next to me. "He has a great voice."

"An *amazing* voice," I said.

"He's a performer, isn't he?"

I smiled. "You could say that."

"Sorry," he said, smiling sheepishly. "I guess I'm not very up-to-date on my celebrities these days. I just got back from an eight-month mission trip with my church."

"Oh, well that's really nice."

"Yeah, I –"

The organs began to play again, and after the music died, the minister gave his eulogy. When it was over, they announced that there would be a private reception at the golf resort that Carol had frequented, right after the burial service.

"Are you going to the cemetery?" asked the stranger next to me as we stood up.

"Uh, I'm not sure," I replied, as he followed me out of the church.

He put his hand to his lips. "I'm sorry, I hope I'm not bothering you. It's just that I don't know anyone here, and Carol was my mother's friend. Mom was too sick to attend, and made me promise to pay my respects."

"Oh, of course," I smiled. "I understand, and you're really not bothering me."

"Good. I also want you to know that I'm not trying to hit on you or anything. That would be horribly blasé. Besides," he lowered his voice. "I'm gay."

I should have known by his mannerisms, but my mind had been on Ransom. "Good to know," I said as we walked out to the parking lot together. "I have to be honest with you, the last funeral I was at, someone *did* hit on me, so I'm sorry if I seemed a little... standoffish."

He looked horrified. "Oh, honey, I'd react the same way." He stuck out his hand. "I'm Julian, by the way."

I shook it. "I'm Tiffany."

"This is me," he said, pointing to a white Mercedes. He dug into his pocket, and pulled out his fob. "Well, in case you *do* show up at the reception, I'll buy you a drink. That way we can keep an eye on each other, and make sure nobody hits on us. Unless, he's tall, dark, and handsome. Or can sing, like Ransom." He sighed. "What I wouldn't do for a night with that tall drink of water."

I bit back a smile.

His face turned red, and he looked up at the sky. "Sorry, Father. I shouldn't be talking like this at a funeral." He turned back to me, a ghastly look on his face. "I'm normally not like this. A pervert. You must think I'm crazy."

I touched his arm. "No, Julian, not at all. Tell you what, I'll meet you at the cemetery, and let you know about the reception. I haven't made up my mind yet on that one."

"Okay."

I smiled. "And, if you're lucky, I might even introduce you to Ransom."

His jaw dropped. "You know him? I should have known. A gorgeous kid like you. Yes, if you could introduce us, I'll try to keep my tongue in my mouth."

"Meet you at the cemetery," I said with a chuckle as I started towards my car.

"Okay."

My cell phone chirped, and I dug it out of my purse. When I noticed it was Remy, I answered right away.

"I didn't see you," she said. "Did you make it the funeral?"

"I was in the back row. It was a beautiful service," I replied, getting into my car.

She sighed. "Yeah, it was. I still can't believe she's gone."

"I know. At least Taylor is by your side now. That's has to help."

"Mm... I suppose."

Her response wasn't very encouraging. I wondered if she was still angry with him. "Is he still in hot water?"

"When isn't he?" she mused. "Anyway, speaking of Mr. Showbiz, I showed him a picture of you, and he remembers your audition. He thinks you have a great shot at making it into the finals. And obviously he knows what he's talking about, Tiff."

My heart soared. Taylor really thought I had a shot? Now *that* was encouraging. "He really liked my singing?!"

"He also said that under no circumstances are you to go near Ransom. Stay as far away from him as possible. If you do and the network catches you, you'll get kicked off faster than you can blink. Just like I've been telling you all along."

"But –"

"No buts. Once the show is over, if you still want to hang out with Ransom, have at it. But if you really want a shot at this, you have to play by the rules like everyone else. He's a *judge*."

"I know."

"It would look like you're cheating!"

I sighed. "Yes, I know. You're absolutely right."

"Okay, enough about the show, and my brother. Are you coming to the reception after the burial?"

"Should I? I wanted to, but if you think it's a bad idea…"

"No, it should be fine. In fact, Ransom said he's not coming, under the advice of Sonia, his agent. It would be too chaotic, especially with all of mom's friends arriving. There isn't enough security, and she doesn't want it turning into this big fiasco. Besides, women from miles away will show up, trying to get their hands on him if he makes an entrance. I feel bad, but it's the way it is."

"Oh. Well then, I guess I'm coming."

"Sounds good. I'll meet you at the cemetery."

After we hung up, I started the engine, and wondered when I'd get to see Ransom alone again. Although I was still excited about the contest, I was still questioning what was more important to me, my dreams of being a singer, or my dreams of being with him.

Chapter Twenty-Two

Ransom

Tiffany stood out like a white rose in the midst of all the black and gray at the cemetery. I wanted to go to her, take her hand in mine for comfort, but I knew she'd be angry if acknowledged her in any way. So I kept my distance, and weathered through the service alongside my sister and Taylor. Thankfully, Sonia was a rock and stood by me through everything, and I decided that whatever Icon was paying her, it wasn't enough.

When the service was over, Taylor turned to me and held out his hand. "I'm sorry for your loss, Ransom. She was an amazing woman."

I shook it. "That's something we can both agree on."

He nodded, and for once, I thought he was actually being sincere.

I turned to my sister, who had tears streaming down her cheeks, and pulled her into my arms. "Love you, Rem."

"Love you, too, Ransom," she choked, clutching onto me. "And... we'll get through this."

"We will," I answered, staring at Tiffany, who was talking to a guy with blonde hair. Our eyes met, and she smiled sadly.

"Are you going to the reception?" asked Remy, backing away.

"I'd like to, but like I said before, Sonia thinks it's a bad idea," I replied.

"Well, Tiffany can't make it either," she whispered. "And security isn't very tight. If I were you, I'd skip it. If you show up, we'll have a stampede of young girls trying to get close to you. It will be a total nightmare."

I nodded. "Yeah, I guess I'll just go home then."

"That's the smartest choice for everyone, Ransom," said Sonia, stepping beside me.

"I suppose."

She leaned into me, and whispered. "While you're there, try to get your hands on that contract of yours. I'd like to go over it with you tomorrow, before you leave for New York."

"Okay."

"By the way, you were incredible today," she said, smiling. "Your mom would have loved hearing you sing that song."

"Thanks."

She nodded and walked away.

I turned to look for Tiffany again, and noticed her walking away from the site with the blonde stranger, and wondered who he was.

"I hate to say this," said Taylor. "But, I still haven't gotten rid of this migraine. Hon, would you mind if I had our limo drop me back off at the hotel?"

She frowned. "Can't you take something for it?"

"I already did. It isn't working. I think I just need to get some rest. I've been running ragged the last few days."

"Okay, at least you were able to get back here for the funeral," replied Remy.

He kissed her on the lips. "I'm sorry I couldn't get away sooner."

She nodded. "It's okay. I'm sure you're hands are tied, with the show, and all."

"You've got that right," he replied.

"Give me a call in the next few days," I told Remy. "Let me know when you'll be back to go through mom's things, and I'll see if I can help."

Her eyebrows shot up. "You seriously *want* to help?"

"Of course. I'll do whatever I can. I mean it, Rem."

"Okay. I'll call you."

I gave her another hug, and then turned to Sonia. "Let's go."

After the limo dropped us back off at my condo and Sonia left, I tried calling Tiffany, but she didn't answer. I then sent her a text, which she took her time responding back to. When she finally did send me a message, it was to inform me that she was at the reception, which surprised me since Remy had said she wasn't going. She also told me that Taylor had issued a warning about being seen with me. She then wished me "luck" in New York.

"Fucking Taylor can kiss my ass," I muttered.

I sent her another text, telling Tiffany that I'd meet up with her later, at her apartment.

My phone rang. It was her.

"Ransom, you know that's a *very* bad idea."

"I think it's a very *good* idea. Who's going to find out? Come on, just one more night together," I prodded.

"I can't." She lowered her voice. "I promised your sister that I'd stay away from you during the contest. Besides, we're going out after the reception. For a few drinks."

I sighed. "That's perfectly fine, I'll swing by afterwards."

"I have no idea what time I'll be home. She mentioned me staying overnight at her hotel, and catching up before she catches her plane tomorrow."

"So, that's it? You've used my body and now you're going to blow me off? Damn girl, I see how it is," I teased.

"It's not like that, and you know it," she replied, a smile in her voice.

"Then prove it," I said. "Come on, let me see you. Please?"

"I –"

Just then Remy got on the phone.

"Ransom, is that you?"

"No. It's Jake, from State Farm."

She snorted. "Leave Tiffany *alone*. You're going to get her disqualified from the show. Is that what you want?"

"What I *want* is really none of your business."

"But that's where you're wrong. I'm looking out for Tiffany's best interests, especially since she's too enamored by a superstar like you to think straight. I'm keeping her with me the entire night, so don't think about trying to hook up with her."

"When did you become such a bitch?" I asked incredulously. "Was it after meeting Taylor?"

"Ha, funny."

"Let me talk to Tiffany."

"Oh... you have to go?" she said, raising her voice a few octaves. "I'll tell her you said that. Have a great night, Ransom."

"Remy!" I barked into the phone.

She hung up.

Furious, I chucked my cell phone across the room. Unfortunately, it hit my bottle of water, knocking it over. I watched in frustration as my phone got wet and the light flickered out.

***

Tiffany

"He really said that?" I asked.

We'd retreated to a private lounge area in the golf club after Remy had spent an hour mingling with the guests, and accepting their condolences.

Remy handed me back the phone. "Yes, I think he's finally coming to his senses. He said to

201

have fun, and that he'll see you on the show next month."

"Oh," I replied, a little disappointed. Although it was for the best, I'd secretly hoped he'd ignore my protests and show up at my apartment later.

"No pouting," she teased. "Hey, here comes Julian with your drink."

I turned around and smiled as he handed me a glass of white wine. "Thanks."

"You're very welcome," he said and then touched his chest. "Damn, you girls need to check out the bartender. Talk about delish. Which reminds me," his eyes twinkled. "Remy, you really look like you could use a refill."

She laughed. "You read my mind."

He pointed to her glass. "What is that, a Cosmopolitan?"

"Yes, but please get me something without alcohol, like a diet soda. I'm taking Tiffany out after the reception, and one of us needs to drive straight."

"Where are you two going?"

"There's a new club in Inglewood that a colleague of mine owns," replied Remy. "We're just going for a couple of drinks on the way back to the hotel. You can join us, if you'd like."

"Oh, I wouldn't want to impose."

"No, it's okay. In fact, if you're with us, then there's a better chance that we won't get hit on," she replied.

He feigned a look of shock. "So, you're using me?"

She smirked. "Not any more than you're using us to get close to that *smexy* bartender, again."

He burst out laughing. "Okay, you've got me there. He's making me drool."

I laughed. "Seriously, though, we would *not* be using you, Julian. Remy and I have both enjoyed your company, especially under these circumstances."

Remy sighed. "Yeah, she's right. I know that I seem like I have it together right now, but I feel like I'm in some kind of dream. That none of this is real."

His eyes softened. "I truly am sorry for your loss, Remy."

She nodded and her eyes became glossy. "Thanks. Great, now I'm going to cry all over again."

I put my arm around her shoulder. "It's okay to cry, Rem. It's not good to keep your emotions bottled up so much. You don't have to be so strong all the time."

"I don't know what I'd do without you," replied Remy. "Especially with Taylor being so busy right now."

"Where is that hunky husband of yours?" asked Julian.

She sighed. "He had a migraine. He went back to our suite."

"I get those," he replied. "I actually get sick to my stomach, they're so bad."

"Taylor seems to have them more and more these days. Especially around me," she said dryly.

My eyebrows shot up. "What? Do you think he's faking them?"

"I hope not. But, to tell you the truth, it's definitely crossed my mind. He never suffered from them when we first started dating."

"How long ago was that?" I asked.

"Almost a year."

I took a sip of my drink. "I'm sure the show is taking its toll on him. All of the traveling and interviews."

"That's what he keeps saying," she replied.

"What show is that?" asked Julian.

"American Icon."

His jaw dropped. "That *was* Taylor Blake! I thought it might have been, but I wasn't sure. Mom never mentioned anything about him being here."

"He's my fiancé," replied Remy.

He rubbed his chin. "And both Taylor and Ransom are on American Icon. I thought I read somewhere that they didn't get along too well."

She smirked. "Well, well, the tabloids actually got something right."

"This is all very fascinating," replied Julian. "And I would love to join you girls, just to hear more about Ransom and Taylor. In fact, I'll even volunteer to be the designated driver, since I'm not much of a drinker anyway."

"Really? You wouldn't mind?" asked Remy.

He waved his hand. "*Mind?* I've been out of the country for the last few months. I need this almost as much as you do."

"Where were you?" asked Remy.

"I was in Belize, on a mission trip. I volunteered at the orphanage."

"That's so very admirable," she replied. "I wish I had the courage to do something like that."

"All it takes is love and commitment. Anyway, it's the least I could do," he said, putting his hands in his pockets. "Plus, I learned a lot about myself. It was a very humbling experience."

She turned to me. "Dammit, Tiffany, why are all the good men gay?"

I laughed.

"We're either gay or married," he replied, chuckling.

"Actually, I've met a lot of *bad* married men," she replied.

"So, why *are* you getting married then?" I teased.

"So when I'm not at the office, I have a man to fuck me when I get home," she drawled.

"Dear, you *have* heard that married couples have *less* sex?" remarked Julian.

"That must count for engaged couples, too," she replied. "Because we hardly have sex anymore, either."

"And marrying him will make it *better*?" I asked, taking a sip of wine.

"Good point," she replied, grabbing her purse. "On that depressing note, I think I'll have a drink. Maybe a Sex-On-The-Beach? If I can't get it in the sand, or my bed, I may as well get it in a glass."

Julian and I burst out laughing.

Chapter Twenty-Three

Ransom

Ignoring their warnings, I grabbed the keys to my Porsche, and decided to take a trip to the golf club. Fortunately, I was able to dodge my security, and leave without getting frisked on the way to my car.

When I arrived at the reception, it was just after eight. I scoped out the parking lot until I found Tiffany's car, and then parked several spots away. I turned off the engine, but left the tunes on, eager to see her one last time before I left town. I didn't even care if we made love or watched one of her chick-flicks. I just wanted to be near her.

I lay my head back against the seat, and pictured the way she'd looked up at me when we'd made love the last time. The pleasure on her face, and the way her lips opened as she moaned. I wanted to see that again. I *had* to see that again. It was driving me insane.

You're falling for her, taunted a little voice in the back of my head. *Admit it.*

Who was I kidding? I'd already fallen, and landed *hard*. This girl was the only thing real in my life. Something I wanted for *myself,* and as far as I was concerned, not even Icon was going to take her away from me. Not if I had anything to do with it.

As I considered my future, and watched for her, other guests began to leave the building.

Just as I was trying to decide whether I should just go in and let her know that I was around, I heard Tiffany's laughter echo through the darkness.

"Julian! You're crazy!" she giggled.

I sat up straight, and watched as that blonde guy from earlier gave Tiffany a piggy-back ride towards her car. They were obviously very comfortable together.

He set her down next to her car and then said something.

They both burst out laughing.

I lowered the window more, and tried to listen.

"I'll drive," he said, grabbing her keys. "We'll just leave my car here."

"Okay. But what if you get lucky tonight?"

He chuckled. "I'm not going to need my car then, am I?"

"Very true. You know, if anyone deserves to get laid after all this time, it's you. In fact I'm going to make sure you do," she rambled, her voice thick. "Nobody should have to wait two years."

"Shh…" he laughed. "Someone's going to hear you."

"I don't care."

I stared at them in shock.

He opened the passenger side door for her and she got in, smiling up at him.

I felt like someone had hit me in the chest with a baseball bat, and then kicked me in the balls. Twenty-four hours ago, she'd been mewling like a kitten underneath me. Tonight, I was being replaced with a guy that looked like a Ken doll.

As they rolled out of the parking lot, I released my white-knuckled grip on the steering wheel and drove to the nearest liquor store, to get numb.

Chapter Twenty-Four

Six Weeks Later…

Hollywood

Tiffany

"This is Taylor Blake coming at you *live* from American Icon!" he said, beaming into the camera with his famously luminous smile. He held up the fingers of his left hand. "Ten-thousand auditions, five major cities, now reduced to thirty hopefuls, all competing to win a seven-year contract with American Icon, which includes a one million dollar sign-on bonus, and a record deal to launch the career of their dreams. What more can I say but let's find us a superstar!"

The familiar music echoed throughout the dressing rooms as the final touches were applied to our hair and makeup. There were fifteen women sharing the same dressing room, and I was scheduled to perform a duet with a male singer, Darren Stryker, who I'd been practicing with all week. The song was from one of Ransom's albums, called, "I'm Over You." The irony of it was, I hadn't heard from Ransom since the funeral, and I couldn't stop thinking about him. Every time I caught a glimpse of his face, or heard his name mentioned, my stomach did flip-flops. I missed him so much, that I could barely concentrate on the contest.

"So, you nervous?" asked the girl, teasing my hair. Her name was Mindy, and she was about my age, with short red hair and green braces.

I held up my hand, which was trembling. "You could say that."

She smiled at me in the mirror. "Look towards the crowd in back. I heard that helps. It makes everyone a big blur."

I wasn't sure if that was going to help me. The fact that I was going to face Ransom again, while trying not to dissect a song from his bestselling album, was making me nauseous. I pictured his cocky grin, the tilt of his head as he watched me perform a hit that *he* was famous for, and I felt like running for the hills. "I'll remember that," I said, trying not to hyperventilate.

She spritzed my hair with something and then sighed happily. "We're done. What do you think?"

I stared at myself in the mirror, hardly recognizing myself. My hair was big, she'd applied a ton of black liner, and my lips were red and glossy. Personally, I looked like I was about to perform in a porno instead of a singing contest. "Uh, thanks."

She glanced down at my short, strapless dress, which was white with pearl sequins. "If the song doesn't do it for them, this dress will. You look amazing."

I stood up, and wondered how they expected me to move easily in a dress so tight, I couldn't even bend. "Thanks."

She giggled. "Just don't fall in those heels. I swear, one of these days, someone is going to trip and fall flat on their face."

"I hope to God that you didn't just jinx me," I said, staring down at the white stilettos.

A woman with deep worry lines on her forehead stuck her head into the dressing room. "You're on in five minutes, Tiffany. Your partner is already waiting near the stage entrance."

"Thanks."

"Relax and break a leg," said Mindy, moving next to me.

I looked down at my heels and winced. "I just might."

"You'll be fine," she replied, urging me forward towards the exit. "Now, get out there before you miss your cue."

"Right," I answered, walking towards the stairs on wobbly legs. Although I'd worn high heels since I was thirteen, these puppies were definitely made for looks, and not for comfort.

"You look beautiful," said Darren, as I met him by the steps. He was in his late twenties and reminded me of an older Justin Bieber.

"Thanks," I said, feeling myself begin to perspire. I could hear the crowd clapping as the last contestants finished their song, and I prayed that I'd make it through the song without puking all over my dress.

"We've got this," he said, squeezing the side of my arm. "Don't worry about a thing."

"I wish I had your confidence."

"I'm confident because of my partner. I feel like a goofball next to you. Your voice is incredible."

I blushed. "Thanks. You really do have a great voice, Darren. Don't ever doubt yourself."

"Easier said than done."

"I hear you."

A man with a clipboard waved us up to the stage entrance. "Come on. Come on."

Darren grabbed my hand, and led me up the stairs. "Those shoes are dangerous."

"I know. They weren't my idea."

"Try not to fall."

"Try to catch me if I do."

He laughed.

"Listen, as soon as they draw the curtains, get into position," said the stage-hand.

"Yes, we know," replied Darren.

Seconds later, the curtains came down, and the other contestants flew past us, full of excited adrenaline.

"Remember," said Darren as we stepped onto the stage. "You're here because your voice was better than thousands of other contestants. We were meant for this. *You* were meant for this."

I swallowed the lump in my throat, and nodded vehemently. "Right... okay... I'll be fine..."

We took our positions on the stage, and each grabbed a microphone. As I turned it on, my pulse went from overdrive to mach-five. I closed my eyes, and tried to steady my breathing as I listened to Taylor on the other side of the curtain, joking with the judges. There was some laughter from the audience, and then he proceeded to introduce us.

Darren winked at me.

The music to our song began to play, and I exhaled.

Chapter Twenty-Five

Ransom

I leaned forward as the familiar chords of "I'm Over You" began to play. When the curtain opened and I saw her standing there looking frightened, but stunningly beautiful, it took my breath away.

Darren opened his mouth and began to sing.

You think you know… me.
You think own… me.
My heart…
My soul…
But the damage is done.
Girl, it's time to move on.
You can't hurt me no more.
I've picked my heart off the floor.
I'm over you…
I'm over you…
Baby, I'm over you…

She smiled, and sang her verse.

I see you smiling at me,
You still don't believe,
That I'm free…
From your chains…
See babe, I don't need you no more,
I've finally made it to shore,
Now this life is my own,

It's time to move on,
I'm over you....
I'm over you...
I'm so over you....

Then they sang together.

Take your lies...
They're always the same...
It's no disguise...
You take pleasure from pain...
But see the joke is on you...
Yeah, I'm so over you...
I'm over you...
Babe, I'm over you...

The song continued with both of them dancing together and singing their hearts out. When it was over, the crowd gave a standing ovation, and I closed my eyes. I'd lost her once, and this was going to separate us even further. If she didn't hate me before, she would now.

***

Tiffany

The judges were in the shadows next to the stage as we sang Ransom's song, which helped ease my terror and anxiety. As the lyrics flowed from my lips, and the tension left my body, I soon found myself enjoying the performance, which surprised the hell out of me. It also helped to see

the smiles of approval on the audience's faces.
When we were finished, and they stood up,
clapping and screaming, I felt like I was on top of
the world. My eyes filled with tears and I couldn't
wipe the smile from my face. I didn't think
anything could bring me down from the cloud I
was dancing on. That is, until I noticed the
expression on Ransom's face.

Scorn.

Taylor walked onto the stage and stood
between us. He grabbed both of our hands and
raised them up into the air.

The crowd began to cheer even louder, and
I forced a smile, trying to ignore the effect of what
his obvious disapproval was doing to me.

"Wow," said Taylor, after he released our
hands. "That was amazing. Both of you."

"Thanks," we replied in unison. I smiled at
Darren who was also grinning from ear-to-ear.

"Judges?" said Taylor, turning towards the
trio. "What do you think? Do these two have what
it takes to get to the next round?"

Deidre awarded us with a beaming smile.
"Are you kidding? It was spectacular. The fans
loved it! *I* loved it!"

The audience roared again, and my cheeks
began to burn, my smile was so wide. When the
noise died down, Tyrone began to speak. "Okay,
so here's what I think. Darren, you were right on
spot, man. Right on spot. Tiffany, you were pretty
tight, too. You reached those chords like a
champion, girl. I have to tell you, though, when

you first started singing, you looked like you were ready to pass out."

I raised the microphone. "That would have been easier."

The audience laughed.

He chuckled. "The winner of American Icon needs to have stage presence. That person has to own the song, the stage, and the entire audience. My advice to you is… relax. Have fun. You're here to perform and entertain, but that doesn't mean you can't enjoy yourself as well."

"Thanks," I said. "I'll try harder the next time. I promise."

He nodded. "I'm sure you will, girl. You already showed us that you can relax up there, over time. You just have to do it *before* you hit the stage. Now, I know that the viewers are in charge of the votes, now, but from where I'm sitting, I think we all know you two are going to the next round. You did very well."

The crowd clapped, and then began to chant *'Ransom'* as the cameras rolled to him. I lifted my chin, and met his hard gaze with as much pride as possible.

"What's wrong, Ransom?" asked Taylor, chuckling. "You don't seem very… impressed."

Ransom smiled arrogantly. "Honestly? I wasn't."

The crowd began to 'boo' him, and his smile widened, obviously not caring.

"Why do you say that?" asked Taylor, putting an arm around my shoulders. "Is it because you're not used to a female singing your song?"

"It has nothing to do with that," he replied. "They missed some of the lyrics, and both of their pitches were off several times. No, I really think it could have been performed a lot better."

"So, what's your opinion? Do you think they should make it to the next round?"

Our eyes locked and his were cold. "Sorry, if my vote mattered, it would be a definite 'No'."

Chapter Twenty-Six

Tiffany

My eyes were stinging as we left the stage. Fortunately, I'd been able to hold the tears, but the moment we were away from the judges and the watchful eyes of the audience, it was Niagara Falls.

"What a fucking jerk," muttered Darren, handing me a tissue. "We *rocked* that song. I know we did. Hell, everyone else knows that we did."

I wiped my cheeks. "I thought so, too."

"The guy has a reputation for being an asshole." His face darkened. "You know what? I bet he gets paid to say 'No'. He certainly says it enough."

"You're probably right," I said, although I knew the truth. He still wanted me *off* of the show. I just didn't understand the animosity in his eyes. Unfortunately, now that the show had started 'live and on television', we weren't allowed to make personal phone calls or leave our hotel, so I couldn't even talk to Remy about it.

"Well, they'll count the votes tomorrow, so there's no reason to let it bother us tonight."

"True," I said, clearing my throat.

He smiled sheepishly. "I don't know about you, but I'm starving. Do you want to eat together tonight? After they send us back?"

"Sure," I replied, looking at the clock. We still had another hour before we could leave, and although I wanted nothing more than to go back to my hotel room and pout, I didn't want to hurt Darren's feelings.

"I'm going to change," I said, staring down at my shoes. "My feet hurt, and I can barely breathe in this dress."

He smiled. "I don't think a lot of the male audience could breathe when they saw you on stage."

I blushed.

"Uh oh, made you blush," he teased.

"You have a habit of doing that."

"I know. It's part of my charm. At least that's what my wife says." He sighed. "I miss her and Julia. I can't believe they won't even allow us a phone call. Not even one!"

Julia was his two-year-old daughter. I'd seen pictures of his family, and it was more than obvious that he loved them dearly.

"Did you see them in the audience?"

His face lit up. "Yes. It was the best part of the evening. I couldn't hear them but my daughter was blowing me kisses. It brought tears to my eyes."

I'd also caught a glimpse of Sinclair, Reed, and Jesse in the audience, and it had felt really good knowing they were there, supporting me. They'd waved, and then during Ransom's speech, I noticed Jesse flipping him the bird with both hands until Reed put a stop to it. It would have been comical if I hadn't been so devastated.

"Only a few more contests to go until the winner is selected. What are you singing next week, if we aren't voted off?"

"Oh, we'll make it. You know, I don't know what song I'm doing yet. They wouldn't tell me," he replied. "Do you know what's in store for you?"

Besides Ransom's scowling face?

"No. I have no idea either. I'm sure we'll find out soon enough."

"Yeah."

"I'm going to change; I'll meet you by the exit when it's time to go."

"Okay."

I hurried back to the dressing room, changed back into my street clothes, and then talked to some of the other girls.

"Did you hear about that guy, what was his name...? Yolanda?" asked Cindy, one of the other contestants.

"Yolanda?" I asked.

"That transvestite. Anyway, he didn't make it to the final thirty, and is trying to sue Icon, saying that he's being discriminated against because of race and sex."

An image of the tall Amazonian came to mind. Jesse's acquaintance. "I met him, actually. He doesn't like taking 'No' for an answer. I saw it first-hand."

"I guess he's missing now," said Cindy, lowering her voice. "And Yolanda's family is claiming that Icon had something to do with it."

My eyebrows shot up. "What? Why?"

"Because of the negative publicity, and the fact that he may have had a good case. I don't know any more except that he's been missing for three weeks, and they're worried."

"I haven't seen anything in the news," I said. Although, I hadn't had time to watch the news.

"I saw something about it," replied Sara, another contestant who was removing her nail polish. "They mentioned it on Entertainment Now. I didn't think anything of it, though. I mean it sounds like a bunch of crap. They're acting like Icon sent out a 'hit' on him. Give me a break."

I thought it sounded pretty ludicrous myself. "I wish I could talk to my friend, Jesse. He knows Yolanda. He might have heard something."

"I can't believe they won't let us communicate with anyone until the show is over," said Cindy. "Not even a phone call."

"It's ridiculous," said Sara. "My boyfriend just got back from Iraq, too."

"How long was he gone?" I asked.

"A little over a year," she smiled. "At least I got to see him in the audience with my mom. I wanted to jump off the stage and throw myself at him."

"I know what you mean," said Cindy. "My husband is taking care of our two boys while I'm away. I'm just glad they're old enough to realize that I haven't abandoned them."

Just then, one of our chaperones stepped into the room. "Show is over. You ladies can get on the bus when you're ready. We're leaving in thirty minutes."

"Thanks," I replied, grabbing my purse.

"Is it just me or does anyone else feel like we're being treated like children?" said Cindy.

"It isn't exactly what I expected," I replied. "But I keep telling myself that it's just a small price to pay for fame and fortune."

"If you *win*," she replied.

"As far as I'm concerned, making it to this point has already been a win for me," I said. "Even if I don't go all the way, I've gotten this far, and I'll never forget it."

"You're one of those 'cup is half-full' kind of gals, aren't you?" smirked Sara.

I shrugged. "Yeah, I suppose."

Cindy smiled. "Can you blame her? She looks like a supermodel and has an amazing voice." She looked at me. "Maybe you can just try and seduce Ransom into taking you under his wing if you don't get a record deal. I heard he can be easily persuaded if you spread your legs wide enough."

My eyes widened. "Oh?"

"Rumor has it he's banging two of the makeup artists. Switch hits every night," said Cindy.

I felt like someone had sucked the life out of my heart and left nothing but a deflated raisin. "He is?"

Sara laughed. "Yeah, I heard Tyrone call him 'Randy Ransom', in the studio earlier when the cameras weren't rolling."

"Randy?" I asked.

"Yeah, as in oversexed," said Sara. "Anyway, it's not a surprise. He's hot, he's famous, and he has women following him everywhere."

"I'd never let him touch me. I mean, you'd really have to be naïve to get into bed with a guy like that. Not only is he a player, but he doesn't care about anyone but *Ransom*."

She was obviously right.

Chapter Twenty-Seven

Tiffany

I joined Darren in the banquet room of the hotel for dinner. They'd set up a large buffet for all of the staff and contestants on Icon.

"At least they're feeding us well," he said, as we went through the buffet line.

"Thanks," I said to a young chef who sliced a piece of prime rib, and placed it on my plate. "No kidding, I would have already gained ten pounds by now, if we weren't burning it off at practice every day."

"Exactly."

We sat down together at a large oval table, not yet occupied, and Darren put his napkin on his lap. "Damn, that was intense today. In fact, I could really use a beer after that performance. Just one. I say after we eat, we sneak over to the bar and have a quick drink."

I raised my eyebrows. "I didn't think we were allowed to stray from the group."

He leaned forward. "We'll just play stupid. Larry Kiel told me that he and Mark Donovan have stopped there every night the last couple of weeks, and nobody has said anything."

I had to admit, a glass of wine sounded really good. "Okay. I never read anything in the rules that said we couldn't drink anyway. So, I can't imagine we'd get into too much trouble, even if someone noticed us."

"There you go."

After we finished eating, Darren and I walked down the hallway to Khol's Grille, which was dead. We sat at the other end of the bar, facing the entrance, and each ordered something to drink.

"Oh, my friend, I've missed you," said Darren after taking a long swig from his beer bottle. "Man, it's funny how you take things for granted when it's suddenly *unavailable*. I'm not much of a drinker by nature, but the fact that I can't just walk into a bar for a quick beer with my friends, is irritating."

I smiled. "I know what you mean. Sometimes after work, I like to enjoy a small glass of wine. It relaxes me."

"That's right, you're a hair stylist. Do you enjoy it?"

I nodded. "It's the people that I work with that make it really enjoyable, though. We have so much fun together." I sighed. "I can't believe how much I already miss them."

"Well, I'm sure they're probably more like family to you."

"You've got that right. I'm the youngest in the group, and they all treat me like the 'little sister'."

"That's good, especially now with your mom being gone. You're too young to be alone."

"Funny, I sure feel old these days," I replied, taking a sip of wine.

Darren looked up and sucked in his breath. "Oh, fuck."

I followed his gaze, and all of the blood rushed to my ears.

Ransom.

And he wasn't alone.

One of the makeup artists from the show was with him. A tall girl with long, red hair, breasts that were barely restrained in the T-shirt she must have borrowed from her baby sister, and a skirt that barely covered her crotch.

Stunned, I looked down at my wine, wishing I could disappear under the floorboards.

"I didn't know the judges were staying at this hotel. Maybe he won't even notice us."

"Let's hope," I whispered.

He chuckled softly. "The girl he's with is pretty distracting. I think we're safe."

I raised my eyes and immediately met Ransom's icy ones. The darkness in his gaze chilled me to the bone. With a scowl, he grabbed the girl's hand and moved to the other side of the bar, ignoring us.

"Phew," sighed Darren, putting a hand on his forehead. "I'm beginning to think he might be doing something that he's not supposed to be doing, either. That's probably why he didn't bust us. "

I drank down the rest of the wine, and stood up. "I'm leaving," I said, feeling slightly dizzy. "Now that he's here."

He slammed back the rest of his bottle. "Okay, let's go."

I grabbed my purse and tried not to cry as I thought about Ransom and his date. Obviously the rumors *were* true, and he didn't give a crap about me. He was, in fact, a male slut.

Darren stood up and we quietly made our way to the entrance. Then, because I just couldn't help myself, I looked back over my shoulder at Ransom, who was staring back at me coldly.

"Whoa," said Taylor, as I slammed into his chest. He grabbed my elbows, and steadied me. "In a hurry, Tiffany?"

"Oh, my God," I said, covering my mouth. "I'm so sorry, Taylor. I didn't even see you."

"Don't worry about it." He cocked and eyebrow, and then looked at Darren. "What are you two doing in the bar?" he teased. "Isn't this place off limits?"

"We just stopped in to see what it looked like," I said quickly.

He laughed. "Relax, I'm not going to say anything. Anyway, I'm glad we bumped into each other. This is perfect."

I smiled. "Oh?"

"Yes, I was wondering if we could have a moment alone, to talk? It won't take very long. I promise."

"Of course." I turned to Darren. "I guess I'll see you tomorrow then, on the bus?"

"Sure. Have a good night, Tiffany," he replied, kissing me on the cheek.

"Thanks, you too."

He glanced at Taylor curiously, and then walked out of the bar.

"I'll just escort you back to your room," said Taylor. "And we can talk along the way."

“Uh, sure.”

We stepped out of the restaurant, and towards the elevators.

“So, how are you enjoying the show so far?” he asked, as we stopped in the hallway.

I pushed the “Up” button and then stepped back. “Well, it’s obviously been pretty crazy. But in a good way.”

“Even with Ransom giving you a hard time?” he asked as the bell chimed and the elevator door opened.

I stepped inside, and turned to him as he followed. “Yes. I mean, he has his own opinion, obviously, about my singing. Which he’s entitled to. At least the other judges are being kind.”

The doors closed and I pushed the number “Ten.”

“So, pardon my frankness, but Remy said that you and Ransom had something going on around the time of the funeral.”

I shrugged. “Not really. I mean we hung out and talked a little. I also cut his hair.”

“You know that wasn’t very smart. You could have been disqualified, even for just ‘talking’.”

I nodded solemnly. “I know. Thanks for not saying anything. I really appreciate it.”

The elevator door opened on my floor, and he followed me off. “I guess that’s what I wanted to talk to you about. Keeping silent.”

I stopped in my tracks. “What do you mean?”

He touched the side of my arm. "How much does winning Icon mean to you?"

The hair stood up on the back of my neck. I took a step away from him. "What are you getting at?"

Taylor smirked and I shuddered as his eyes raked over my light blue blouse, which suddenly felt uncomfortably revealing. "I've risked a lot by keeping my mouth shut. You were at the funeral, you had some kind of intimate relationship with one of the judges, and now, I just caught you breaking another rule." He reached forward and tucked a strand of hair behind my ear. "I think you know where this is going."

Horrified, I tried to play dumb. "Look, I'm sorry that you feel like I've placed *you* in some kind of awkward situation. I truly am," I said, backing up. "But I'm not trying to get you into any kind of trouble, Taylor."

He lowered his voice. "I know you're not trying. But, my job could be in jeopardy if things get leaked."

"But *you* didn't do anything. If anyone is going to get into trouble, it would be me or Ransom."

"No, I'm pretty sure that my ass would be canned if the media gets wind of this. Now, I've kept my mouth shut, and let me tell you, it's been very stressful. So stressful, in fact, that I think I should be compensated in some way. For risking my own neck."

"I have no money," I said, staring at him in disbelief.

He smirked. "I know that. I also know you're naïve enough to think I'm talking about money."

"Excuse me?" I asked, truly repulsed by him. I couldn't believe this worm was engaged to Remy.

His eyes slithered over my body again. "Invite me back to your hotel room where we can discuss this more intimately."

I turned and walked towards my room. "You've got to be kidding."

He followed me. "Tiffany..."

I stopped at my door, and pulled the room key from my purse. "Just get away from me, Taylor."

He leaned his shoulder against the wall and regarded me with amusement. "So, I guess that means you don't really care about getting kicked off of the show?"

"I'm *not* going to get kicked off of the show," I snapped.

"Don't be so sure of yourself, *Taffy*," he snapped back. "Think about it. You have *nobody* on your side right now. Ransom has obviously forgotten about you. Remy, well, if she finds out that you were sleeping with a married man, Darren, she's going to be mortified, even more so when I tell her how you tried to seduce me just so that I'd help you advance to the finals."

I stared at him in horror. "What?"

"The choice is yours – one night with me, and the rest of the show will be smooth sailing. I'll protect you from the media and any inquiries regarding Ransom."

"You're my best friend's fiancé. How can you even think that I'd agree to this?"

He rolled his eyes. "Oh, grow up. You're not in Kansas, pumpkin. This is Hollywood, and that's how we do things here. You want to get ahead, you have to give a little... head."

I pushed the door open and turned back to face him. "Hollywood or not, I will *never* have sex with you or give you a blow job, you fucking prick. Hell, I'd rather get kicked off of Icon." I glared at him. "And by the way, you don't know the kind of friendship Remy and I have. She would *never* believe your lies. But, she will believe the truth when I tell her how you tried to get me to sleep with *you*. I'm going to make sure she leaves your ass so fast, you won't know where to find it."

With a sneer, he grabbed my shoulders and pushed me backwards into my hotel room. "You'd better think about that before you open your big mouth," he growled, staring down into my face. "Don't fuck with me, because I'm always going to fuck with you harder."

I took a step backwards. "Get out of my room."

He smiled coldly. "First, you're going to promise me that you won't say anything to Remy."

Ransom stepped through the door, grabbed Taylor, and threw him up against the wall. "You prick," he growled, putting his hand around Taylor's neck. He pulled his fist back. "I should beat the fuck out of you!"

Taylor, who was much smaller than Ransom, tried uncurling his fingers with little success. His face went from red to purple as he struggled to breathe.

"Let him go," I begged, afraid that he'd kill Taylor and end up in prison. "It's not worth it. Don't do this."

Ransom, who was breathing hard, grunted, and then reluctantly released Taylor's neck.

Taylor gasped and leaned over, putting his hands on his knees as he tried to catch his breath.

Ransom stared down at him with disgust. "I should fucking kill you, man. You cheat on my sister, and try this shit with Tiffany?"

"You don't know what you're talking about," replied Taylor in a raspy voice. He stood up and pulled at his collar. "I should sue you for attacking me."

"Go for it," snapped Ransom. He then smiled coldly. "Hell, you know what, if you're going to sue me, I may as well make it worth my time."

I watched in shock as Ransom's fist slammed into Taylor's face.

"Fuck!" he hollered, doubling over.

"Now walk the fuck out of here," ordered Ransom. "Or so help me, I'll hit you so hard again, that you'll be crawling."

Taylor, whose eye was already starting to puff out, opened his mouth to respond, but then apparently thought better, and stormed out.

Chapter Twenty-Eight

Tiffany

Ransom turned to me, his face still dark with anger. "The next time you invite a guy up, make sure he's not married, or an asshole like Taylor. Tonight you obviously got a two-for-one."

My jaw dropped. "I didn't *invite* him up to my room! He said he wanted to talk, and proceeded to follow me onto the elevator. I had no idea he was going to try getting me into bcd."

"Right. I find that hard to believe."

I stared at him in exasperation. "Frankly, I don't care *what* you believe. You've been a total prick to me, and as far as I'm concerned, you need to haul *your* ass out of my room, too!"

He took a step towards me, his eyes flashing. "Why, because *Darren* is on his way up?"

I glared back at him. "No! Of course not. Anyway, shouldn't you be downstairs with *your* little cupcake? Or did you just get lost on the way to another girl's room?"

He smiled coldly. "Do I detect a little jealousy?"

"No!" I sputtered. "As far as I'm concerned, you can fuck whoever you want! I don't give a crap!"

"Is that right?" he said, staring down into my eyes, looking so arrogant I wanted to punch *him* in the face. "You really don't care?"

I clenched my fists. "No I don't. As far as I'm concerned, you can go fuck *yourself* while you're at it, too."

The look on his face might have frightened me if I hadn't been so angry with him myself. "Is that right?" he asked, now breathing so hard, he reminded me of a fuming bull.

I pointed towards the door. "Yes. Now leave. Go fuck the entire makeup crew of Icon if you want. I couldn't care less."

"Liar," he growled.

Before I could answer, he pulled me into his arms, and his lips crashed against mine, hard and demanding.

Gasping, I gave in to the rush of lust that took me by surprise. I slid my arms around his neck, and pulled him closer, my anger replaced with lust.

We staggered together, his tongue in my mouth, and my fingers in his hair, pulling and tugging in desperation as I tried to get closer without losing my balance. When his hands gripped my hips, I could feel his erection pressed against me, and I dragged him towards the bed, where we fell together.

He sat up with me on his lap, raised my blouse, and tossed it aside. Then his hands slid to my breasts, squeezing, while his mouth moved to my neck.

Grinding my pelvis against his hips, I closed my eyes and reveled in the feel of his hard cock pushing against me.

Ransom's lips moved lower, and he unclasped my bra, squeezing both of my breasts, then bringing them to his mouth. I moaned in pleasure as he sucked and rolled one of my nipples between his teeth while the other hand moved between my legs. He wasn't exactly gentle, but it turned me on even further.

"Let's get rid of these pants," he said, rolling us over until he was on top. Soon, they, along with my drenched panties, and his T-shirt, were gone.

He stared down at me, and then repositioned himself between my legs, pulling my knees over his shoulders. He turned his head, kissing and nipping at the soft skin on my inner thigh making my legs tremble. As his lips moved closer to my heat, I grabbed onto the sheets, anticipating his hungry mouth on my slickened folds. Instead, he stopped. "Tell me you care," he demanded, placing a finger near my opening.

"Yes," I whispered back. The truth was that I cared, more than I ever wanted to admit.

He stared up into my eyes, and then began to wiggle his finger.

"Oh," I moaned as he watched my face, his eyes dark with desire. Then he slid it deep inside of me, and lowered his mouth.

I gasped in delight as his tongue began to move along with his finger, fast and relentless. After only a few seconds, my lower stomach tightened, and the fluttery tingle between my legs grew until it exploded into an orgasm that brought me to tears.

"That's it," he murmured. "Let's see if we can give you another."

Just then, someone started knocking on the door.

Ransom's head shot up, and we stared at each other in the darkness.

"Tiffany?"

Crap. It was Darren.

Ransom's face darkened, and he sat up.

Sighing, I turned to get out of bed, but he apparently had other ideas. He grabbed me around the waist, and pulled me onto his lap. Pushing the side of my hair away from my neck, he bit my earlobe. "Where *are* you going?" he whispered. "I'm not finished, yet."

"Tiffany?" hollered Darren. "I could have sworn that I heard you screaming. Are you okay?"

"Uh, I'm getting ready for bed!" I yelled. "I'll talk to you tomorrow."

He paused. "Are you okay?"

Ransom pushed me forward, until I was on my knees, and then kneeled behind me.

"I'm fine," I answered as he unzipped his jeans, and rubbed the tip of his cock against my opening.

"You sure? You sound funny."

"Yes," I replied breathlessly. "Don't worry about me."

"Well, okay. Goodnight."

"Night."

"So beautiful," whispered Ransom, running his hand down my back. "God, I've missed you."

Tears sprang to my eyes as he replaced his hand with his lips, kissing my spine, his lips more tender than before. "I missed you, too."

"I've never wanted anyone like you, Tiffany," he said, pulling my hair over my shoulder. He leaned forward and kissed my neck. "You're all I ever think about. Us together. You in my arms."

"Me too," I whispered, turning my head.

He brushed my lips with his, and then straightened up. "I've been dreaming about being inside of you for the last few weeks," he said, squeezing my buttocks.

I spread my legs wider. "Then quit dreaming."

He grabbed my hips firmly, positioned himself, and then plunged into me from behind, both of us moaning in pleasure at the tightness. As he began to move in and out, I closed my eyes and reveled in the sweet sensation of what it was like to be filled by Ransom. Panting, I opened my eyes back up and glanced over my shoulder at him as he thrust into me, harder and deeper.

"Yes," I panted as his hips moved faster and the pressure began to build inside of me with each thrust.

Harder.

Deeper.

I moaned.

He leaned forward and brought his hand to my sex, rubbing it as he plunged in and out of me from behind until I peaked and then soared into hot oblivion, moaning in ecstasy.

Ransom gasped and shuddered against me as my pelvic muscles contracted around his shaft. Still leaning over me, he squeezed my breast firmly, and held me against his chest, as he came, pulsating inside of me.

I closed my eyes and smiled.

I was in heaven.

I was with the only man I wanted to be with.

I was also leaking something between my legs.

I stiffened up. "Ransom?"

"Yeah."

"Uh, did you use a condom?"

He didn't answer.

I turned around and looked at him. "I could get pregnant, you know, among other things."

He smiled innocently. "Could you just imagine the talent in our child?"

I scowled. "This isn't funny. I'm way too young to be a mother. Plus, you're not exactly *father* material."

He looked hurt. "What do you mean?"

I got out of bed and ran a hand through my hair, forgetting about my nakedness. "This is insane. What in the hell were we thinking. What in the hell were *you* thinking?"

"I'm sorry," he said. "I was too caught up in the moment to think about a condom."

"You must be carrying one in your wallet. I mean, what were you going to do with 'Red'?"

He frowned. "Red?"

"The girl in the bar? The one with the big... you kno..."

He stared at my chest. "Tits?"

I glanced down, and my cheeks turned red. "Yes," I replied, grabbing the blanket from the bed. "The girl who was showing more skin than a newborn."

Ransom laughed. "She's married to one of my band members. There's nothing going on between us, Taffy."

"Well, rumor has it that you're screwing two girls. Two hair stylists," I sniffed.

He folded his arms across his chest. "At the moment, I'm only screwing one, and she's making a fool out of herself."

My jaw dropped. "Making a fool out of myself?"

"Look, I haven't had sex with anyone since you."

I nodded towards the alarm clock. "That's good because you haven't left the room yet, and it's only been five minutes."

Ransom chuckled.

"I don't see what's so funny."

He got out of bed and then reached for me. "Would you chill out?"

I slapped his hand away. "I can't do this, Ransom. I keep picturing you with other women. You have this horrible reputation and... and you haven't called me or... tried seeing me," I said, raising my chin.

"So? That was then, before I fell for you, Taffy. And yeah, I've wanted to see you, but you told me to stay away."

He had me there.

"You've never listened to me before, though," I replied. "When I asked you to stay away."

He sighed. "Listen, the night of the funeral, I snuck out of my condo and went to the reception to surprise you, but I saw you leaving with that blonde guy." He scratched his head and frowned. "What can I say, it really pissed me off."

"Julian?"

He shrugged. "I have no idea what his name was. I saw him giving you a piggy-back ride, and you enjoying yourself. I figured, you'd already forgotten about me."

"Julian is just a friend, and he's... gay."

His eyebrows shot up. "Gay?"

"Yes. Gay."

He groaned. "Fuck."

I grinned. "Were you jealous?"

He grabbed me around the waist and pulled me into his arms. "Yes. I was ready to jump out of my car and beat the fuck out of him."

"I'm glad you didn't. Julian is a really nice guy. He spent several months volunteering at a mission. I think you'd have secured a spot in Hell after doing something that bad."

He snorted. "Babe, my spot is already reserved. When you've sinned as much as I have, redemption isn't in the cards anymore."

I scowled. "First of all, don't get me started on that. There's always hope and you can turn your life around. Second, you've got to stop trying to control my life."

His eyes widened innocently. "Control your life?"

"Yes. What do you call trying to get me kicked off of Icon?"

"I call it saving your ass from making a bad mistake," he replied with a smug smile.

I pushed him away. "Dammit, aren't you ever going to give up?"

"I'm trying to save you from Icon, a different kind of hell."

I groaned. "God, I'm an adult. I should be able to make my own decisions."

"That's what I thought, too. Haven't you noticed how controlling these bastards are? You're basically locked in your room; you can't speak with anyone outside of the show. You can't have a damn beer without getting a permission slip. Tiffany, this is just a glimpse of what you'll be subjected to if you win this show."

"Fine, but let me decide what I want! Quit trying to put up roadblocks, and making me feel like a failure on stage." My eyes filled with tears. "You have no idea how much that hurt today. Here, I thought I did a pretty good job, singing one of your songs, and you crushed me, Ransom."

His eyes softened. "I'm sorry..."

"Well, then stop this! I mean, did you even *like* how we performed?"

He smiled. "Hell, I couldn't have sang it better myself."

I slugged him. "Then tell me! Make me feel proud, like I accomplished something! All I wanted was to see you nod or give me the thumbs up. Maybe even to say *'good job'*, Tiffany. Instead you made me feel like a total loser. It was humiliating."

He stepped closer. "I'm sorry. I didn't mean to hurt you. I just want to save you from –"

I shoved him backwards. "You're a broken record, Ransom. Look, it's obvious I can't win this fight with you."

"Then let's *not* fight. I'll help you get a record deal with someone else. I have connections. I can hook you up."

"That's just it. I don't *want* your help. I want to do this on my own. I want to know that it was my voice that landed me a record deal, not because I know you."

"They won't sign you unless they think you're talented, anyway." He stared down at me. "Come on, Tiffany, let's just pack our stuff and forget Icon. Sonia has found a way for me to get out of my contracts so I can walk away, clean and clear. I'm going to start fresh, see if I can convince my old band members to take me back. Write my own music, make my own decisions, and get my life back." He smiled. "I want you with me."

"I'm really happy for you, Ransom." I sighed. "But, I've invested so much in this already. Let me just finish up the contest. If I win, you can help me find a lawyer who will negotiate my contract."

"It's not that easy."

"It might be."

Ransom's cell phone began to ring. He reached down and picked it up. "It's Sonia. I've got to call her back and find out what she's learned from our lawyer."

I nodded. "Okay."

He leaned over and kissed me on the lips. "I swear, I'll bring condoms next time. Scout's honor."

I laughed. "You'd better."

He pulled on his clothes while I grabbed my robe from the closet. When he was finished, he sat me on his knee. "I'm sorry about the judging. I swear to God, I've never wanted to hurt you. I've only wanted what was best."

"It's not up to you to find out what's best for me," I said. "You have to let *me* figure it out."

He put his lips against my forehead and whispered, "I know."

Chapter Twenty-Nine

Tiffany

Fortunately, both Darren and I made it to the next round on Icon. We were interviewed together on the show the following day, by Taylor, who acted like nothing had happened. When the interview was finished, he pulled me aside, and apologized.

"I'm so sorry about last night," he said quietly. "I'd been drinking and... to be honest, I really feel sick about the whole thing."

I didn't say anything. Something about the look in his eyes didn't hold true to his words.

"You're not going to mention this to Remy, are you?"

Disgusted, I shook my head and walked away.

Ransom snuck back to my hotel several times during the following week after practice. We spent most of the time in bed, and when we weren't making love, we played cards, talked about our families, and made up lyrics for new songs.

"I had no idea you hadn't written any of the songs on your albums," I said, after swallowing a forkful of Lo mein. "I just assumed that since you used to write all of your old stuff back in high school, that you'd written the new stuff, too."

"No. I wasn't allowed to contribute any of my stuff," he said, tapping his pencil against his notepad.

"What happened to your old music?"

"I'm assuming it's where I left most of it – in my old bedroom. Unless my mother had packed it away."

"Speaking of which, have you talked to Remy?"

He frowned. "Actually, I tried talking to her about Taylor, but as usual, she refused to listen. She thinks that I hate the bastard so much, I'd make up anything."

"Do you hate him?"

He smirked. "Do you have to ask?"

"I can't stand him either. I can't believe she really thinks that you're lying. God, I can't wait to talk to her. She'll have to listen to the both of us."

"I hope she kicks his ass to the curb," he said. "And I get to watch."

"Me too."

He leaned over and kissed my nose. "I'm liking that even more. You and me. Together."

I smiled.

He leaned back. "If you win Icon, you'll be traveling quite a bit."

Oh, here we go.

"I know."

"It's not as glamorous as you may think. I mean for a guy, it's not really that bad."

"What's the difference?"

He chuckled. "I don't think I have to spell it out for you."

I smirked. "Oh, you mean because of the partying and loose, skanky women?"

"You could say that."

"I'm sure there are many female artists who enjoy partying and loose men while on the road."

"Just for the record, all men are loose, babe."

My eyebrow arched. "Is that right?"

He burst out laughing. "But not all men are available."

"That's better."

"So, have you decided if you're going through with the song tonight?"

"Why wouldn't I?"

He leaned forward. "Because you were thinking about quitting the show?"

I clucked my tongue. "You just don't give up, do you?"

"Of course not."

"Are you going to vote 'No' tonight?"

He stood up and walked towards me. "Depends on how good you are."

"I'm serious."

He smiled. "I'm serious, too."

I stuck my tongue out.

"Do that again," he replied, touching his zipper.

"Not if you're going to vote against me," I teased. "On purpose."

He dropped his hand and sighed. "You know how I feel about this show."

"I thought you were going to let me make my own decisions."

"You can and nobody is stopping you. Speaking of decisions, I also have a very important one to consider. Now," he said, looking at the clock. "I need to make some phone calls. I'm sorry, babe, but I won't get to see you until you're actually onstage tonight."

I frowned. "Why do the *judges* get to make phone calls, but contestants aren't allowed to make even one?"

"Because, you're contestants. You might leak information."

"So could the judges."

"True, but not as likely. I suppose it's just easier for them to monitor three judges than it is for thirty contestants. Besides, we're under contract. We say anything and we could get sued."

I snorted. "Yeah, and we all know how *you* follow the rules."

He smiled.

"It still makes me mad."

"It's Icon. Like I said, this is just the tip of the iceberg. If you get chosen, you won't be able to shave your bikini line without getting permission. Speaking of," he smiled wickedly. "I like what you've done with the place."

My cheeks turned bright pink. I'd been bored one night and had decided to give myself a 'Brazilian'.

He leaned over and kissed me. "I love the way you blush even more."

"You're incorrigible."

"Thank you."

"It wasn't a compliment."

He wiggled his eyebrows. "For me it is."

I smiled and rolled my eyes.

He picked up his T-shirt from the ground and pulled it over his head. "So, what song are you singing tonight?"

"It's a surprise."

"Not going to tell me, huh?" he asked, grabbing his phone from the nightstand.

"No and if you tell me I suck, I'm going to jump off of the stage, and kill you."

He feigned a look of shock. "You do know that threatening or bribing a judge is not only against the rules, but illegal?"

"If I go to jail," I said, opening up my robe. "Will you pay me a conjugal visit?"

He dropped his phone on the floor, picked me up, and tossed me on the bed. "You wicked, wicked girl."

Chapter Thirty

Tiffany

"You're up next, Tiffany."

I stared at myself in the mirror and felt a sense of calmness that I hadn't felt in the last few weeks.

"You look exquisite," remarked the makeup artist, Rene, who had a slight French accent.

Our eyes met in the mirror. "Yes. Thanks again for not overdoing the eye makeup."

He smiled. "Eyes like yours look better without."

"Thanks," I replied, standing up.

Tonight I had on a long, red dress that tapered to my waist, showed a hint of cleavage, and flowed down to a small train. I felt like I was ready for the Oscars.

"Be careful you don't step on the dress," he said, helping me spread the bottom out.

"I'll try."

This time my red heels were only two inches, nothing compared the previous week when I wobbled in the other ones.

"I'll walk you to the stage," he said, lifting the back of my dress off of the floor.

"Thanks," I replied as we were escorted towards the stairs leading to the back of the stage. When it was my turn to take position, I started getting another panic attack.

"What's wrong?" asked Rene, straightening out the train again.

"Nerves," I said, waving a hand frantically by my face, trying not to sweat.

"Just remember, you are beautiful and you sing like an angel. Nobody can take that away from you."

I smiled. "That is so sweet, Rene."

"Actually," he smiled sheepishly. "I agree with the sentiment, but these words are not from me. I have something for you." He reached into his suit pocket, pulled out an envelope, and handed it to me.

I opened it up and read the message.

You are beautiful and sing like an angel. Nobody can ever take that away from you. I love you, Taffy. I just wanted you to know. R.

My eyes filled with tears as the realization of how much I loved *him* made my heart swell. Truthfully, I'd already known that I'd fallen in love with Ransom, especially during those weeks he'd stayed away and I'd missed him. Not seeing him had killed me, even though it was what I'd requested. Now, to know that he had *real* feelings for me, it was a wonderful feeling.

I grinned stupidly.

Ransom loved me.

"Sorry," said Rene. "I was told to memorize it, in case I couldn't hand you the envelope. It was important to him that you knew."

With a squeal of joy, I threw my arms around Rene and hugged him. "Thank you."

He chuckled as I pulled away. "Well, I think I need to be the postman more often."

I wiped a couple of tears from under my eyelashes. "Is my makeup, okay?"

He tilted his head and nodded. "Are you kidding, you look beautiful."

"Rene, get off the stage!" hollered one of the crewmen. "Vite!"

Rene saluted him, gave me a wink, and then scurried from the stage.

The audience clapped as the judges finished giving their opinions on the performer before me.

My pulse raced. I was up. I took a deep breath.

This round, we'd been given the freedom to select a favorite love song. The song I'd chosen was the one I used to listen to as a teenager, when I'd lie in bed at night, fantasizing about Ransom. Now, it truly represented everything I felt in my heart. He was, and always had been, the man of my dreams.

As the curtain began to open, I took another deep breath, and allowed myself to relax.

"Tiffany!" the crowd roared, and began to clap.

I smiled.

Then the familiar music began to play. I raised the mike and directed most of my attention towards the dark silhouette of the only judge in the room that mattered.

The whispers in the morning
Of lovers sleeping tight
Are rolling like thunder now

As I look in your eyes

I hold on to your body
And feel each move you make
Your voice is warm and tender
A love that I could not forsake

'Cause I am your lady
And you are my man
Whenever you reach for me
I'll do all that I can

Lost is how I'm feeling lying in your arms
When the world outside's too
Much to take
That all ends when I'm with you

Even though there may be times
It seems I'm far away
Never wonder where I am
'Cause I am always by your side

'Cause I am your lady
And you are my man
Whenever you reach for me
I'll do all that I can

We're heading for something
Somewhere I've never been
Sometimes I am frightened
But I'm ready to learn
Of the power of love

The sound of your heart beating
Made it clear
Suddenly the feeling that I can't go on
Is light years away

'Cause I am your lady
And you are my man
Whenever you reach for me
I'll do all that I can

We're heading for something
Somewhere I've never been
Sometimes I am frightened
But I'm ready to learn
Of the power of love

I lowered the mike, and the audience stood up, clapping and calling out my name.

The rush was incredible.

I brushed away the tears under my lower lashes, as Taylor walked towards me, a fake smile plastered across his face. When the clapping stopped and the lights grew brighter, I stole a glance towards Ransom, whose expression was stoic.

"*That* was amazing," said Taylor. "I think if Celine Dion herself were in the audience, she'd be giving you the thumbs-up."

"Thanks," I replied, my face flushed from seeing the grins and even a few tears on the audience staring back at me. Then, when I noticed a sign that read: "We love you, Taffy!" and

Jesse's and Sinclair's beaming smiles below it, I raised my hand to my lips, and blew them a kiss.

"Deidra," said Taylor, turning towards the judges. "What did you think of our 'lady' tonight?"

Her eyes were shining brightly. She clasped her hands together and nodded. "Tiffany Banks. You know, you just keep getting better and better, my dear. That was superb. I don't think you could have sung it any better. Cheers."

"Thank you," I said. "That means a lot."

She tilted her head. "Well done. I know in my heart that you'll be voted to the next round."

"I hope so," I replied.

Taylor spoke into his mike. "Tyrone, what about you?"

"I've said it before, Tiffany Banks has the talent to go all the way. She's beautiful, talented, and America loves her. I don't know about you guys out there," he looked back towards the crowd, "but when she stepped out of the shadows and opened her mouth, I wanted it to be *me* she was singing to."

Claps erupted in the crowd and I felt my cheeks turn red as a guy in the audience howled.

"Thanks, Tyrone," I replied.

"You keep it up, girl. You've got what it takes."

"I hope so."

"Ransom," said Taylor, his voice slightly strained. "Are we going to get another 'no' from you, or has she finally proven herself to our most critical judge?"

The crowd grew quiet.

Ransom and I stared at each other. I smiled but he didn't return it, nor did he give *anything* away in his expression. "Ms. Banks. I want to say that your performance tonight was crap... that it was horrible, that you should forget this contest, and walk out the door because you just don't have what it takes to win. I would really, *really* love to say that."

The crowd began to 'boo' him.

He raised his voice. "*But*, I'd be doing you a grave injustice." He smiled. "You blew me out of the water, and so far away, that I'm still trying to find my bearings."

I exhaled and began to breathe again.

"I've never heard anything so amazingly beautiful in my entire life," he said, his own eyes glimmering. "You deserve everything you want in life, whatever it is. *You*, beautiful lady, deserve to go all the way, and there is really nothing else to be said."

The crowd stood up and clapped, chanting "Ransom." He lifted his hand and waved at the audience, a big smile on his face.

I raised the mike to my mouth. "I disagree, Ransom. I think there is definitely more to be said."

He leaned back and stared up at me in confusion.

Taking a deep breath, I tossed away the mike, picked up the train of my dress, and headed towards the edge of the stage, where the judges were all seated. I lowered myself down and then ran to where Ransom sat, shocked as hell.

"Taffy?" he asked, standing up. "What are you doing?"

Tears filled my eyes. "I love you, Ransom, and I don't care about this contest or anything else, for that matter," I said, launching myself at him before the surrounding security guards had a chance to stop me. I threw my arms around his neck and kissed him hard on the lips.

Stunned, the crowd went wild and began to clap.

"I love you, too," he replied, wrapping his arms around my waist when I came up for breath. "Tiffany Banks."

Chapter Thirty-One

Tiffany

Obviously, I was kicked off of the show. So was Ransom. He was ecstatic, and well, I didn't care either. I had what I wanted, Ransom, and it was more than enough. Plus, I'd received several offers from other record producers interested in hearing me sing, none of which were associated with Icon, so my musical career wasn't over quite yet. Funny thing was, it just didn't seem as important as it did before, so I decided to hold off for a while.

Instead, I returned to the salon while Ransom moved back to his mother's house with his sister. Unfortunately, after breaking his contract, he lost everything, including the support of his band members, all of his property, and the rights to the songs that had really made him famous. In other words, he was broke. A real starving artist. But, in all honesty, I'd never seen him so giddy and excited, especially after he started practicing in his parents' garage again, with the old members of his band, the *Soul Bandits*. The ones he'd grown up with. They'd buried the hatchet, and although most of them had careers now, they were all eager to jump back into the swing of things, especially after Sonia, Ransom's agent, started negotiating deals with other record companies still very much interested in him. This time he made a solemn promise to his old friend, Robby, that he'd never abandon the band again.

It would be all or nothing.

Remy broke it off with Taylor, after we'd finally convinced her of what a real shit he was. In the end, she'd admitted that it hadn't been that much of a shock, considering he was away so much, and that she wasn't getting any sex when they *were* together. Instead, she started hanging out with Julian, who eventually talked her into signing up for a mission trip to Uganda during Christmas. It had shocked the heck out of me, but I knew it would be good for Remy to get away and focus on helping those who were so much less fortunate then her.

Ransom and I spent all of our free time together, and although I'd offered to let him move in with me, we both decided not to jump into anything. At least until I turned twenty-five. He hinted that it would be a good age to get married and have kids.

"To you?" I'd asked.

"Unless you want to ask Jesse," he'd replied with a smirk. "I'm sure *that* honeymoon wouldn't go over well."

Needless to say, my life was wonderful. I had Ransom, my friends at Tangled, and the memories of the standing ovation I'd gotten on Icon. Right now, it was all I needed.

Then, six weeks after being kicked off of Icon, I was sitting in the break room at Tangled, stuffing my face with the leftover pizza that

Ransom had brought over the night before, when Sinclair sat down next to me.

"Notice anything different on me?" she asked, smiling broadly.

I stared at her face. "Not... really."

She raised her left hand and waved it next to her cheek. "Now?"

My jaw dropped. "Oh, my God! Is that an engagement ring?"

"Yes," she beamed. "Reed asked me to marry him last night!"

"I thought you guys were separated?"

"We weren't *really* separated. I mean, I wouldn't answer his phone calls, or see him for a couple of weeks."

"That sounds like a separation," I replied dryly.

She smiled and stared down at the ring. "Fine. Anyway, he insisted on seeing me last night, and well, gave me this."

I stared down at the large rock. "It is beautiful."

She held it up to the light. "I've never had anything this expensive before. It's overwhelming. All of it."

"So, um, did anything ever happen between him and his assistant? Isn't that what you were so worried about?"

She turned back to me. "He swore up and down that nothing happened. He also told me that he couldn't live without me. *Wouldn't* live without me."

"Do believe him?"

"I do. Truthfully, he didn't give me any reason to think that he was cheating. He's a lawyer and works long hours. He warned me about that. So, his assistant has the hots for him, and is a total bitch, that doesn't mean he's going to cheat."

"Good point."

"Besides," she grinned, "he said he'd let her go if it really meant that much to me."

I leaned forward. "Are you going to make him do it?"

She giggled. "Well, I *wasn't*, but then Jesse called the office early this morning. Apparently they started arguing, and then she hung up on him, really pissing Jesse off. He got ahold of Reed on his cell phone, and I guess he ended up firing her anyway."

I held up my hand and she slapped it. "Nice."

"I know, right?" she grinned. "Now, I don't even have to feel guilty about it."

"The bad thing is he'll need to hire a new assistant and might be busier than before. God, I hope he starts spending more time with you."

Her eyes lit up. "He's going to have to. See, that's the other thing... I haven't even told him yet. I was going to do it tonight."

"Tell him what?"

"I'm pregnant."

I stared at her in shock. "You're pregnant!"

"Shush!" she whispered. "Nobody else knows yet, not even him."

"Congratulations, *again*. How far along are you?"

"Almost three months."

My jaw dropped. "What? And you haven't told him?"

"I was going to but then we had that big fight and separated."

"I can't believe you didn't tell him already! Well, you don't look very pregnant," I said, staring down at her waistline.

"Believe me, I've gained about five pounds already. You're not really supposed to show until you're closer to four months anyway. That's what my doctor said."

"How've you been feeling?"

"Not too bad. I've been a little sick in the mornings, but nothing a few crackers can't fix. I guess I'm pretty lucky."

"I'm so happy for you," I said. "A baby and a ring. You must be overwhelmingly happy!"

She laughed. "You could say that. So, speaking of being happy, what's going on between you and Ransom?"

I sighed dreamily. "Great. Better than great. I really love the guy."

"Do you think you two will get married someday?"

I blushed. "We kind of talked about it. But not now, maybe in a few years."

"That's wise. I wouldn't jump into anything this soon."

"I know. I'm really not ready for marriage right now, but if he asked, I definitely wouldn't say 'No'. It's kind of banned from our relationship now anyway," I chuckled.

She pushed a curl behind her ear. "He seems like a really nice guy. Nothing like the media made him out to be."

"I know. He said that he's a changed man."

Felicia stepped into the break room. "You have a call on line two, Sinclair."

"Oh, maybe it's Reed," she said, her eyes sparkling. "He's getting off early. Oh, my God, I'm so nervous about telling him."

"Nervous about what?" asked Felicia.

She paused. "About telling him what I want for my birthday," she lied.

I smiled. Felicia would tell everyone if she found out. She couldn't hold a secret and was the first to admit it.

Felicia frowned. "It's a guy on the phone, but definitely not your man Reed."

Sinclair picked up the phone on the table. "Hello?"

I watched as her face crumbled.

"What's wrong?" I whispered, staring the hand that held the phone. It was trembling.

Her eyes filled with horror. "You leave me alone or I'll call the police, you sick son-of-a-bitch."

Whoever was on the other line said something else.

She slammed down the phone.

"Who was that?" I asked.

She clutched her stomach with both of her hands. "I... I need to find Reed. Oh, my God..."

"What's wrong? I asked. "Who called you?"

Her lips trembled. "It was that freak that kidnapped me last year. Michael. Oh, my God, he isn't dead…"

The End